W9-AQG-277

DISCARD

now you see it...

now you see it...

Richard Matheson

A Tom Doherty Associates Book

New York

NOW YOU SEE IT . . .

Copyright © 1995 by RXR, Inc.

This book is printed on acid-free paper.

A Tor Book
Published by Tom Doherty Associates, Inc.
175 Fifth Avenue
New York, N.Y. 10010

Tor ® is a registered trademark of Tom Doherty Associates, Inc.

Design by Lynn Newmark

Library of Congress Cataloging-in-Publication Data
Matheson, Richard
       Now you see it— / Richard Matheson.
              p.   cm.
       "A Tom Doherty Associates book."
       ISBN 0-312-85713-6
       I.   Title.
    PS3563.A8355N69   1995
    813'.54—dc20   94-4107
                                            CIP

First edition: February 1995

Printed in the United States of America

0 9 8 7 6 5 4 3 2 1

To my dear friend Robert Bloch,
who created magic in all our lives

Magician's Choice: A technique in which two or more choices are supposedly offered for free selection by the spectator but a predetermined one actually is imposed upon him.

magician's choice

chapter 1

Daresay you've never, in your life, read a story written by a vegetable. Well, here's your chance. Not that it's a story. It happened; I was there.

Your narrator and humble servant, Mr. Vegetable.

My name is Emil Delacorte. When all this occurred, I was seventy-three.

You've probably never heard of me, even though I was a headlining magician in the 30's, 40's and 50's; called *The Great Delacorte*—a title I passed along to my son. I'm sure you've heard of him.

I was doing very well until I had a "cerebrovascular accident" in 1966. That's a "stroke" to you, though I'm more inclined toward "apoplexy"; sounds more colorful. The experience itself, of course, was not so colorful. Though it was, God knows, plenty dramatic.

To me, anyway.

I was on the verge of being sealed into a boiler tank (one

of my better escapes) when a blood vessel in my brain popped, depriving said brain of oxygen supply. *Hemiplegia* (paralysis) took place, commencing the process which converted me into the aforementioned vegetable.

Quite a vision to my audience, I gather. From charming, urbane Delacorte (The Great) I was suddenly reduced to a dizzy, vertigo-locked, nauseous reeler. No doubt startling to the assembled folks. Disgusting too, as a violent headache and vomiting set in.

Not exactly the highlight of my showbiz career.

Soon afterward, permanent paralysis began, the loss of speech, and my one-way ticket to Vegetable City. Sudden death from stroke being rare, I was not permitted the grace of taking my final bow and exiting the stage of life.

Instead, the best fate could offer me was a doctor's instruction to reduce physical and emotional tension while I waited for as much recovery as possible.

Fourteen years later, when these events transpired, I was still waiting.

By dint of my son's loving kindness, I was not dispatched to some asylum but permitted to reside in his home, a motionless figure customarily located in the study—or, as I prefer to call it, The Magic Room.

There I sat ensconced in my wheelchair, a staring obelisk, an effigy of what I'd been, a statue entitled *Impotence* (in more ways than one) or, better still, *Up On the Shelf for Good.* A voiceless, torpid lump, ostensibly brainless.

───

There, you see, is the rub. For the real torment was that in that dumb shell I existed in, an active and observant brain was struggling for the means to express itself. That is the horror of a stroke, believe me.

Perhaps if this had happened ten or twenty years later,

there might have been some medical-surgical procedure by which I could have ended my night- (and day-) mare.

Then again, perhaps not. Even my son, devoted as he was to me, might have found it inescapable to A&F (Accept and Forget). Who could have blamed the man? I had become more a piece of furniture than a family member. Not hard to take a piece of furniture for granted.

I go on at length about my plant-kingdom persona so you will understand how all these strange events could have taken place in my presence without a single person involved giving it a second thought that I was there. But then, do we concern ourselves with the observational capacities of a turnip?

Anyway, Maximilian (my son) had enough problems of his own, as you will discover.

A few more explanatory comments before I launch into my account of that fateful day.

Because of Maximilian's loyalty to me, I had a nurse (one Nelly Washington) who stayed with me constantly (in the beginning, anyway), providing those attentions I could not request but obviously required—eating and elimination to the fore.

Nelly was no Venus but she had an inner beauty of compassion, a good deal of patience, and (luckily for her as well as for me) an abundant sense of humor. Most of all, God bless her giant heart, she never allowed me to remain defeated or helpless. She was a rock of reassurance on which I wobbled constantly until some semblance of hope oozed back into my brain—along with a few restorative drams of blood.

I'm glad she happened to be absent on the day it all took

place, although in retrospect, I realize that it probably was no accident.

After all, she would have been an obviously sentient witness to the mania which occurred.

━━━━━▭

One thing about residing in a useless body in the sole company of one's brain: it gives one time to appraise said brain, appreciate its true capacities, and, eventually, train it to perform. In this way I was able to educate my brain to remember everything I saw around me, thus enabling me to write down this event in full detail.

This is fortunate because the events I will describe took place fourteen years ago. I will explain, in due course, why I had to wait so long to disclose them.

But first, let me sketch in the environment for the play, or—most appropriately—the setting for the magic show. For magic is the dark thread which binds together the tapestry of this crazed and homicidal episode, this lethal interval of time.

This period of total lunacy.

━━━━━▭

This happened in the home where my son had lived for thirty-seven of his fifty-two years. My wife Lenore gave birth to him in 1928, dying ten years later giving birth to our second (stillborn) son.

As indicated, Maximilian had been (since my "accident" made it impossible for me to perform) *The Great Delacorte*. He had been my assistant since he was seventeen, and knew my act as well as I did, performing on his own as well as continuing to help me, reaching full theatrical bloom when he was thirty-seven and assumed my stage name.

Living in this house were two other people, not counting the houseman and cleaning woman, who were also not present on that day. Coincidence? My aged, wrinkled ass it was.

The first of these two people was Max's wife Cassandra, forty-one, a woman of uncommon beauty, intelligence, and nastiness. She had been married to Max for nine years, his assistant in the act for eight.

Cassandra had two goals in life. One was to get my ancient bones out of the house and into a distant vegetable farm.

The other was . . . well, that must wait, or we have no tale.

The third resident of *Delacorte Hall* (exclusive of Nelly and the two servants, of course) was Cassandra's brother Brian, thirty-five, an employee of my son's.

The house was (still is) in Massachusetts, standing in the center of a twenty-two-acre plot of woodland, set back approximately a quarter of a mile from the road. (Forgive the exactitude of detail, it's a habit I'm unable to overcome.)

Described briefly (I'll try, anyway), *Delacorte Hall* was (is) French Provincial in design, a truly splendid two-story structure which I'd had built in 1943, a choice earning year for me.

The house had (has) seven bedrooms and baths, a modest theater, a swimming pool below, a large kitchen, formal dining room, a large living room, and the rooms in which the hours of insanity took place—my study and, later, Max's.

The Magic Room.

Why do I call it that? Because it was a masterpiece of prearrangements, a cornucopia of gimmicks and arcana. I had begun the process in 1945 for my own pleasure. Later, Max had added to it; so much so that, at the time of these events, even I was unaware of what he'd done to the room, my earlier years of invalidism having been spent in my bedroom. It was only in the late sixties that Max saw to it that Nelly brought my wheelchair on a daily basis to TMR, knowing the pleasure I had always taken in it when I was a real person instead of a two-eyed potato.

<hr>

The study then; *The Magic Room.*

Thirty feet in length, twenty in width, many-windowed with one particularly large picture window affording a spectacular view of the countryside behind the house, a small lake in the distance, a gazebo on its shore.

The study had always been luxuriously appointed. Built-in shelves lined two walls, many filled with leather-bound scrapbooks: my reviews and news clippings, and Max's. The remainder of the shelves were filled with books almost exclusively devoted to magic history and/or methodology.

On a third wall hung framed lobby posters of my and Max's more notable appearances.

A fieldstone fireplace (quite massive) stood against the fourth wall, on its mantelpiece a collection of relics, souvenirs, and *objets d'art* which Lenore and I—and, later, Max—had collected through the years. Also standing on it was a silver candelabra with three black candles, next to it a silver matchbox.

Fret not, dear reader, these details are of consequence, all of them a valid part of the account.

Where was I?

Yes, the fireplace. Above the mantelpiece hung several items.

Two were large oil paintings, one of my lovely Lenore (I blessed my son for leaving it there), the other of an equally lovely (perhaps stunningly beautiful would be more accurate a description) young woman: Adelaide, Max's first wife, who died in 1963.

Also mounted above said mantelpiece was a set of English dueling pistols, circa 1879; a pike from the nineteenth-century Spanish Army; and an African spear and blow-gun—all to play their roles in the murderous exploits soon to commence.

Near the fireplace was my (then Max's) desk, eighteenth-century French, its glossy surface seven feet by four feet, on it an arrangement of relics, souvenirs, and *objets d'art* from my (our) collection. A telephone and a silver-plated decanter (with glass) completed the articles on the desk. Behind it was a high-backed revolving chair, upholstered in black leather.

———

Other items to be mentioned: a handsome brass-and-teakwood bar, glasses and silver ice bucket on its top; two red leather easy chairs with end tables; an extremely large (two feet in diameter) antique world globe.

Finally, a quintet of items vital to the narrative.

One: a standing lobby display poster—a life-size photograph of Max in top hat and tails, a placard reading:

THE GREAT DELACORTE
"In Touch With the Mysterious."

Two: an ornately decorated Egyptian burial case, standing upright, its lid open.

Three: a suit of armor (sixteenth-century German), its faceplate shut.

Four: a lever-operated guillotine (a miniature version of the one used during the French Revolution), its blade raised to the top as though positioned to decapitate some doomed marquis.

Five: set upright on its lever-operated base, a mahogany casket with a window to reveal the head and shoulders of the deceased.

Inside the casket were what appeared to be the head and shoulders of my son—Maximilian Delacorte, handsome (got my looks), vandyke-bearded (an ostentation I eschewed), eyes shut, expression imperious, the very image of a Spanish grandee lying in state.

How's that for memory?

◼️⬜️

Anyway, dear reader, mark these things.

All were integral to the madness.

How shall I typify what happened? Passion play? Somewhat. Weird tale? Indubitably. Horror story? Pretty close. Grotesque melodrama? Certainly. Black comedy? Your point of view will determine that. Perhaps it was a combination of them all.

Suffice to say that the events which took place in the home of my son on the afternoon of July 17, 1980, were, to say the least, singular.

So to the story. A chronicle of greed and cruelty, horror and rapacity, sadism and murder.

Love, American style.

chapter 2

By shifting my eyes to the utmost, I could read the small clock on Max's desk. Eleven fifty-seven A.M. A gray and windy morning, outside sounds—wind, rustling foliage, distant thunder rumblings—harbingers of an approaching summer storm. Nature herself conspiring to set the scene for that turbulent afternoon? Who knows?

I was seated in my usual place, a location chosen by my son from which I could, by (as noted) shifting my eyeballs, get a panoramic view of The Magic Room. I had breakfasted, been changed, and now was in position to observe the many doings about to occur.

Which began, as I recall, at noon. And if it wasn't exactly noon, to hell with it, I'm going to *say* that it was exactly noon.

At noon, the cabal began.

I heard a voice shout, "Cassandra?"

That of Brian (Crane), calling from the entry hall. My eyeballs shifted; pretty much the extent of my physical dexterity, I might add.

There was silence for a few moments. Then Brian called again, more loudly, *"Cassandra!"*

Somewhere upstairs, a door was opened (my hearing, too, was unimpeded) and Cassandra answered with her usual imperious tone, *"What?"*

"Come down to Max's den!" he shouted. "I've got something to show you!"

"Brian, I am really *busy!*" Cassandra shouted back.

Brother persisted. "You can spare a minute! Come on!"

"Brian!" a protesting cry now.

He would not back off. "I guarantee you'll love it!" he shouted.

Reluctant submission from Cassandra. "Oh, all right."

I heard the clicking of a woman's shoe heels on the wooden floorboards of the entry hall—

—and Cassandra entered The Magic Room, tall, blonde, alluring. Long-sleeved pink blouse, light brown skirt, brown, high-heeled shoes.

I would have frowned if my facial muscles had been up to it.

How did Cassandra get here first when she was upstairs and Brian down?

I tried to see more clearly as she crossed to the bar and, stooping, opened the door of the ice maker. I heard her start to ladle ice cubes into the silver bucket.

I would have frowned again—in spades—if I'd been able to.

For, down the staircase and across the floorboards of the entry hall, I heard the clicking of a woman's shoe heels—

—and Cassandra entered TMR, tall, blonde, alluring. Long-sleeved pink blouse, light brown skirt, you know the rest.

"What the hell?" I would have said if my voice had been attainable. I certainly thought it. *What the hell is going on?*

Was I hallucinating now, a new (and lower) stage of stroke-dom?

The moment the second Cassandra had entered the room, the first Cassandra had stopped putting ice cubes into the silver bucket.

I watched the second Cassandra as she looked around, her gaze passing me, as usual, with non-reception. Does one take notice of a plant?

Then the first Cassandra rose from behind the bar and *thrumped* down the bucket on the counter.

The two Cassandras eyed each other, doppelgängers to the detail. I closed my eyes; that I could manage. *When I open them*, I thought, *I'll see only one of them.*

I did. I didn't. There they were, the Cassandra twins. Did I begin to get the message at that point?

If I did, it wasn't because I was helped by either of them.

The first Cassandra smiled.

The second Cassandra smiled—then shook her head with a chuckle.

As did the first.

The sounds they uttered were identical as the second Cassandra indicated amusement, then the first.

There was no way, let me assure you, that I could tell them apart. It could have been double vision. My mind's eye knew otherwise but my skull's eyes didn't.

Now the second Cassandra approached the bar and stopped, peering closely at the first. The first peered like-wise.

The second made a sound of appreciative recognition. The first made the identical sound.

The second gave the first a chiding look. Received it back, identically. The game was getting on my nerves; patience was not one of my virtues at that time, though obviously no one knew it.

Irritatingly, these two were clones in manner as well as appearance.

The second gnawed at the edge of her right index finger, smiling, making noises of amusement. So, too, did the first.

Then the second spoke.

"All right," she said.

"All right," echoed the first.

Their voices were identical.

Damn it, will one *of you crack?* I thought.

The two Cassandras eyed each other saucily, smiling the same smile, affecting the same expression; an uncanny sight, I'm forced to admit.

The second ran fingers through her long blonde hair. So did the first, laughing throatily—as did the second. *When will this damned burlesque conclude?* I wondered.

It had a few more stages to go.

The second Cassandra raised her right hand. The first one raised hers, the movement a duplicate.

With a repressed smile, the second suddenly produced a scarlet handkerchief from the air—a minor "appearance"; sleeve concealment.

The first Cassandra stared at her. The second chuckled, on the verge of triumph.

At which the first, with a duplicate chuckle, produced the same scarlet handkerchief.

The second threw her head back with a startled laugh. So did the first.

Impasse, the twins regarding one another.

Until the second Cassandra tossed her handkerchief into the air.

As did the first.

The second, though, grabbed at hers abruptly as it fell, causing it to vanish.

Despite her efforts to do likewise, the first Cassandra was

unable to prevent her handkerchief from fluttering to the floor.

The second made a sound of victory and pointed at the first—who made a sound which might have been translated as, *"Oh, well, you can't win them all."*

The second clearly examined the first. "Not bad," she allowed.

"Damn perfect," said the first, still with Cassandra's voice.

The smile of the second Cassandra disappeared. "Are you sure he's still out walking?" she demanded.

"Would I be doing this if he weren't?" asked the first, now in his own voice.

"Well, we can't take any risks," Cassandra told him disapprovingly. "You'd better go upstairs and change."

By now, a chill had begun to settle in my stomach as I stared at them.

What are they up to?

"I have to set it up first," Brian was saying, gesturing vaguely toward the room.

Cassandra frowned. "You should have done that earlier," she said.

"With all I had to do?" he answered; again, the coldness in my vitals.

Cassandra grimaced with impatience. "Well, get it over with, but *fast*," she ordered him.

She started to turn away when Brian grabbed her arm, restraining her. Cassandra looked around in irritation. "What?"

"You're determined to do this?" Brian asked.

Now I really felt disturbed.

"Brian, we have gone through this already—*endlessly.*" Her tone was coldly critical, making it obvious that whatever was going on, it was her idea, not his. "Now come *on*," she said. "You have to get out of here." She looked around uncomfortably. "Harry could get here any moment."

"All right." He looked at her, a distressed Cassandra appraising her calmer twin.

Seeing this, Cassandra put her hands on his arms and smiled with reassurance. "Brian. *Darling*," she said. "It's going to be all right. Fear not!"

He did not respond, and *she* looked concerned now. "I can depend on you, can't I?" she asked.

His look and voice were gravity itself.

"Haven't you always?" he said.

She squeezed his arms. "Get *on* with it then," she told him.

She turned and moved to the doorway, shoe heels clicking on the oak floor.

There she turned. "And if you hear Harry's car drive up, or the doorbell rings, for God's sake, get upstairs right away."

"All *right*," he said. He sounded almost angry now. It was the most he could manage with his sister. Anger, he could not permit himself.

He loved her too much.

Before she left, Cassandra did something which intensified the chill inside me.

She looked at me directly—something she never did— and stuck out her tongue. A childish gesture which dismayed me far more than a scowl or a snarl might have done.

"Why don't you leave him alone?" Brian said.

She didn't reply, only gave him a look.

Then she was gone, and Brian was picking up his fallen handkerchief and moving to the fireplace. As Max's assistant, he was expected to complete the preparation of the room. No detail could be overlooked.

The feeling of gratitude I had for Brian's sympathy was

undone by the coldly venomous look he gave to Max's replica as he passed the upright casket.

Cassandra and he had some dark plan with regard to my son. I knew it clearly.

And I could not do anything about it. Do you want to know the sum and substance of true frustration? It was what I felt as I sat there, watching Brian at the mantelpiece while he lifted the silver box, raised its lid, and removed a single match from its interior. Striking the match on the bottom of the box, he began to light the first black candle.

Startled, then, I looked toward the doorway. There had been no car sound and no warning doorbell.

Yet Harry Kendal—Max's booking agent—was striding into the room.

chapter 3

stared at him, a burst of formless hope inside me. *Could this be an answer?* I thought. *A solution to a problem about which I have no knowledge whatsoever?*

Let me describe Harry Kendal; it may help you understand.

He was in his upper fifties, tan, lean and treadmill-fit, his hair profuse and silvery. A distinguished-looking man, but less in the manner of a college don than a Mafia one.

It being July, he wore the accredited New York showbiz uniform—a lightweight, white and blue pinstripe suit, a white shirt and a dark blue tie; nothing but the best in quality of course.

Carried in his right hand was a tropical-weave summer hat, in his left a monogrammed leather attaché case, list price $450 at the very least. Harry Kendal was a man who always did well for himself.

His first words were, "Here I am, babe."

The expression of alarm on Brian's (Cassandra's) face as

he whirled gave me renewed hope. Not knowing, as I've said, what Brian had in mind to do with Cassandra, I hoped that this unexpected surprise might, at least, undo what seemed to be a part of it—his imitation of Cassandra.

So I watched, smiling (inwardly, of course), as Harry, grinning (outwardly), cried, "Whoa! Sorry! Didn't mean to startle you!"

"I—" Brian broke off instantly. Obviously, he knew this wasn't going to work beyond a first brief space of time. He cleared his throat and reproduced his sister's voice again, saying, "I didn't hear your car drive up."

"Took a cab," Harry told him (her). "Walked in from the highway. Just opened the door." His sleazy smile was now in evidence. "Thought I had that privilege."

As he spoke, he placed his hat and attaché case on the chair nearest him and, glancing toward me briefly, raised a limp hand in salute to my irrelevant existence.

I did not return the greeting.

Now he moved toward Brian, who—very abruptly— turned back toward the mantelpiece, his heartbeat no doubt accelerated markedly. (The realization did *my* heart good.) Brian tried to ignite another match, his mind probably fishing for a quick way out of this dilemma.

Harry reacted with a frown of surprise to "Cassandra" turning her back on him and stopped to look at her quizzically. "How you doin'?" he inquired.

I saw Brian swallow nervously; Harry couldn't see it from his vantage point. "I'm fine," he said. Cassandra's voice, of course.

"Where's the Marster?" Harry asked.

"Walking," Brian answered. Was he feeling breathless, giddy? Lord, I hoped so.

"*Glad to hear it*," Harry responded.

I may have imagined it but I think that Brian tightened

even more, hearing Harry's tone of voice with its intimation of "moving in" on Cassandra now that he knew her husband was not about.

Brian glanced across his shoulder, and I felt a rare glow of pleasure as I saw that he saw that, indeed, Harry was moving in on him.

Heart in throat (I trust), he moved quickly to the picture window overlooking the lake and corded shut the drapes. Instant gloom pervaded the room; to Brian's advantage, of course, I realized with a twinge of frustration.

Harry grunted. "That certainly makes the room a lot more cheerful," he said. He watched Brian return to the mantelpiece for another try at lighting those candles. Then he added, "However, it *does* make the room a lot more *intimate*."

I wonder if he heard the faint groan which I heard in Brian's throat. Had Brian made it even worse for himself?

Noting Harry "on the move" once more, he hastily lit the three black candles and, as though he didn't notice Harry's stalking approach, moved swiftly behind the desk and turned on the lamp, the illumination of which was cast only downward.

Harry stopped again, now looking piqued; I enjoyed the sight. "What's wrong?" he asked.

A quick and trembling breath in Brian's lungs. *"Nothing,"* he said.

Then an idea obviously occurred to him; a rare occurrence, I believed at that time. "Listen, I have to go upstairs for a minute—"

His voice broke off in utter shock as Cassandra (who had, fortuitously, put on a pair of noiseless slippers since the shoes she'd been wearing—always too small by dint of vanity—had been pinching her feet) started into the room, a bottle of champagne in her hands.

Never have I seen a faster reaction. Catching sight of

Harry, she whirled with the skill of a dervish and vanished in an instant, Harry never noticing; he was moving toward the desk now, saying, still piqued, "Wait a minute, babe."

He stopped in his tracks as Brian, growing desperate, moved around the other end of the desk and headed for the entry hall.

"*Wait* a minute," Harry told him (her). He was more than piqued now, he was positively pettish.

Brian stopped, not turning; I enjoyed an imagined vision of his heart expanding and contracting like an overdriven bellows.

"What is *wrong?*" demanded Harry.

"*Nothing,*" insisted Brian.

"Well then, turn around for Christ's sake," Harry ordered her (him).

Brian hesitated, doubtless fearing that the game was ended before it could start; whatever the game was. Then, slowly, he turned to confront the stern-faced Harry.

"Look, I don't like this, babe," said Harry. "I took a cab here all the way from Boston just because you asked me. I'm not here to sell encyclopedias." Daresay he thought that was a telling sting.

Brian's spirits must have been flagging by then. "I know," he said. "I'm sorry. I—"

Again he broke off as a panel in the wall behind Harry opened soundlessly (a frippery I'd had installed when the house was built) and he saw—as I did—his sister signaling to him frantically.

Brian, by now, was too rattled to hide his reaction, and seeing Brian's eyes shift, Harry turned to see what he was looking at. *Eureka,* I thought.

Then I scowled (although my face remained the same) as Cassandra closed the panel instantaneously; Harry saw nothing. Scowling (visibly), he turned back to Brian, really angry now. "*What the hell is going on?*" he demanded.

Brian clearly had no glimmer as to what he should say or do. Harry starting toward him seemed to petrify his limbs.

Until, as Harry nearly reached him, a fit of frenzy seized his bones and he moved—lunged might be more the word—to the display poster of THE GREAT DELACORTE and picked it up. "Have to move this," he muttered, barely in Cassandra's voice.

"*Oh, for Christ's sake,*" Harry said, observing Brian carry the poster to the area in front of the moving panel. Abruptly then, he turned away, disgusted. "Screw it, babe," he said. "I'm going back to Boston."

"*No,*" said Brian.

Hastily, he stepped behind the poster. Harry couldn't see, but I could; as the panel was reopened quickly, Brian and Cassandra made the switch and Brian shut the panel. *Damn!* I thought.

Cassandra (now the real) picked up the poster and returned it to its original place. "No," she said, "Max wouldn't want it over there."

That Harry's feeling, at that moment, was no greater than disgruntlement tells you how essentially identical Cassandra and the made-up Brian looked. No doubt a close appraisal would have revealed discrepancies but, from the distance Harry had been—the distance Brian had made sure to keep him at—the similarities far outweighed whatever minor differences in appearance there might have been.

Further, Harry had no notion that Brian could imitate his sister. Accordingly, it would have taken a glaring inconsistency on Brian's part for Harry to even have conceived of it, much less noticed that inconsistency.

Even further, Harry had been so thoroughly ego-aggrieved by Cassandra's snub of him that he'd been in no state of mind to consider physical replication.

For God's sake, the man was so fundamentally obtuse

that he never even noticed how Cassandra's footwear went, in one fell swoop, from high heels to slippers!

———

Cassandra obviously knew those things, because her tone of voice was totally unruffled as she moved to the drapes and opened them. "He really doesn't like the drapes shut either," she remarked, turning back to Harry with a confident smile. Oh, density, thy name is Kendal!

"Finished with your little game now?" he inquired sarcastically.

"*Sweetheart*," said my faithful daughter-in-law.

Turning off the desk lamp, she moved to Harry, slid her arms across his shoulders and planted an intense and lingering kiss on his lips. (Do you require any further evidence that my existence was, to her, no more substantial than the presence of an artichoke?)

Harry's instant physical response was thoroughly predictable and Cassandra knew it, pressing loins and stomach to his calculable groin, his Achilles crotch. I had never known before that moment that Cassandra had been intimate with Harry, but, I must say, the discovery came as no bombshell explosion in my mind.

Cassandra allowed the breathless grinding to go on for a while, then pulled free with a labored exhalation, feigned, I have no doubt. She drew back, grasping his hands in hers. "How *are* you, darling?" she asked.

His response was to glance uncomfortably at me. "Are you sure—" he began.

"He's brain-dead, love," she assured him.

"But his eyes—"

"—perceive nothing; he's no more cognizant than a head of lettuce."

If you had only known, Cassandra.

"How *are* you, darling?" she repeated.

"Provoked," he answered.

"Did I behave badly?" she asked.

"I'd say dementedly," he answered.

"I'm sorry, I just—" She broke off and I thought: *You aren't really going to say it, are you?* But she did! "—haven't been myself today," she finished.

She kissed Harry on the lips again, lightly this time to prevent further excess groin provoking. "I'm sorry, love," she said. "It's everything that's going on here. You understand, I know you do."

A grumbling "I suppose" from Harry, anxious to preserve his macho image even though he'd obviously succumbed to her already.

Another peck to his pouting lips, an imploring look. "I've been so upset," she said.

He patted her back, his ego restored. "All right, all right," he said. He looked around, shaking his head. "This whole *room*," he went on. "It's too damn much. That *casket*, for God's sake. When did he put the figure in it?"

"He wants to know what he'll look like at his funeral," she answered.

"That's *sick*," he muttered.

Her smile was cold. "That's *Max*," she amended.

He looked at her again. "You said he was walking?" he asked.

Cassandra hesitated, then realized that Brian must have said it. "Yes, he is." She nodded.

She reacted as, with an anticipating (ever sleazy) smile, he moved at her again. "He could be back any moment though," she told him quickly.

He frowned, then sighed, accepting. "All right," he said reluctantly.

She took his hands again. "Thank you for coming," she said.

"How could I resist?" he replied. "Your request as well as Max's?"

Cassandra stiffened noticeably. *"He* asked you to come as well?" she asked, clearly taken by surprise.

Displeased, uncomfortable surprise.

chapter 4

You didn't know?" asked Harry.

"No, I—" She could not complete her remark. All she could do was repeat the word "No," her face a mask of disconcertment.

"Well, that's good news, isn't it?" he asked. "It means he's probably changed his mind."

"You really think so?" asked Cassandra. For a moment there, she sounded almost optimistic; about what I had no idea—but then you already know the sum total of my knowledge of events transpiring: zero.

Harry gestured as if to comment, *Why not?*

"Babe, he could have said 'no' on the phone," he told her.

When she failed to respond, he added, "Why ask me all the way up here just to turn me down?"

She remained unconvinced; that was easy to see, even for a head of lettuce.

"I'm sure that's what it is," persisted Harry. He assumed his "serious" mien. "What *about* Vegas, babe?" he asked. "Can he handle it? *Even with you?*"

"I don't know," she murmured. I could tell she was conversing with him and dealing with her thoughts at the same time, a skill she'd carefully developed.

"Was Baltimore as bad as I heard?" he asked.

She was back now, in control; it hadn't been a serious unhinging. She looked at Harry with an expression of deep distress; it almost seemed real—*was* it? "You can't imagine," she told him quietly.

Harry put his arms around her and she leaned her forehead on his shoulder. He stroked her back and told her he was sorry. "It must have been a nightmare," he said.

What is this? I wondered.

"*God*," Cassandra sobbed, and damned if it didn't sound perplexingly genuine. "To stand there on the stage with him, watching him *drop* things."

Oh, now wait a second, my mind protested.

"Watching him miss verbal clues . . . visual clues—*obvious* ones," she went on. "Watching him bungle hand manipulations he could do in his *sleep* a few years ago. Flounder through his performance. *Flounder*, Harry! Him! The Great Delacorte! The most gifted—"

She began to cry harder.

If I hadn't been already speechless, I would have been speechless.

Could this be true?

Max *floundering?* Bungling hand manipulations? Missing clues? My son, Maximilian, *The Great Delacorte?*

It had to be impossible. I didn't think I could endure the pain of it being true.

━━━━━▭

Harry obviously felt helpless before her grief. (I felt helpless myself; it seemed so *real*.) All he could do was pat her clumsily on the back and murmur, "Easy, babe, easy."

"It broke my heart to watch him," Cassandra said, able to

speak once more. She drew in a lengthy, trembling breath, then raised her head and shook it slowly. "Followed by three long months up here, watching him sink a little deeper into despair every day."

I felt myself swallow. Max *had* seemed very gloomy in the past few months. His attentions and words to me had been dispensed with enervated melancholy. I had equated it with his unhappy marriage.

But his *career?*

Now Cassandra clutched at Harry's arms so tightly that it made him wince.

"You're his best friend, Harry," she told him. (There she lost me.) "You're his *only* friend." (Lost me double!) "If you can't talk him into this . . ."

She sobbed, began to cry again. If it was an act, it was of Tony, Oscar, and Emmy caliber.

"Easy, babe," he said. "I think he's changed his mind, that's why he asked me here today. It's gonna work."

She looked at him uneasily. "Did he say anything in particular that makes you think that?" she asked.

"No, but why else would he ask me here?" he counter-questioned. "Like I said, if he wanted to say no, he could have done it on the telephone."

"I suppose." She still didn't sound convinced.

"Has he been to a doctor?" Harry asked.

A *doctor*, for God's sake? Now what were they talking about?

Cassandra's sigh had been a heavy one. "He won't go to a doctor," she said.

"You think he's afraid of what he might find out?" Harry asked her.

She shook her head. "I just don't know."

Harry grimaced. "He's not that old," he said. "What, fifty-one?"

"Fifty-two," she answered.

"That's not old."

"His father wasn't that old either," said Cassandra.

That sent a chill right through me, let me tell you. Had Max also suffered a stroke, albeit a mini? Enough to diminish his physical and mental capabilities?

The thought was shocking to me.

Cassandra had walked to the picture window and was gazing out. "It's going to rain," she murmured. She sighed again and looked toward the desk chair as though Max were sitting there. Another sigh. Moving to the chair, she pushed idly at its high back, making it revolve.

She then began to pace the room, her expression one of mounting anguish. (I hated the ambivalent emotions she was arousing in me.)

"I remember every detail of the night I first saw him," she said. "The Orpheum in London. God, he was magnificent! The most majestic-looking man I ever saw on stage!" Of course, she'd never seen me. "The way he *moved*. The grace—the flow—the total, overpowering magnetism of him! It was awesome! The audience was his slave. And so was I."

She was at the fireplace now, staring into its shadowy depths. She shook her head, a smile of bitter self-reproach on her lips. "But I'm living in the past," she said. "All I see now is a crumbling edifice. A *parody* of what he was." (This was more in keeping with the Cassandra I knew; or, the Cassandra I thought I knew.)

Harry moved to her and put his arms around her once again. She leaned against him wearily.

"He's going to let you do it, babe," he said.

"I don't know that, Harry," she responded.

"Babe, he isn't going to let the whole act die," he said. "He's not a stupid man." (That much Harry had correct at any rate.)

"I hope so," Cassandra murmured.

She straightened up, a look of grim determination on her face.

"I can *do* it, Harry," she declared. "I've worked for years! I'm not saying I'm as good as he is." How modest of her. "But I can *do magic.* I can *do* it."

"Shh. Babe. Easy." Harry was patting her back again. "Am I arguing with you? I want to see you make it too; you know that. I want to see you playing the best clubs and theaters in the country—hell, in the *world!* The first really important female magician!"

Using the act that I—then Max—developed over the past half-century, I thought, a bile of angry resentment aciding my insides.

"It's gonna happen, babe," Harry told her confidently. *Bastard*, I thought.

"I can *do* it, Harry!" she said, her tone a fierce one now. Max really had a battle on his hands, I saw.

"Sure you can," said Harry. "That's why I'm here. To make it happen."

Cassandra visibly calmed herself. She looked at him almost pleadingly. "You're my last hope, Harry," she said. "If it doesn't happen today . . ."

What was going to happen that day was eons beyond what any of us could have imagined in our wildest flight of fancy.

"It'll happen," Harry said though, unaware. "Take my word for it."

She looked hopeful for a moment. "It would be so simple to update the act," she said.

Ah-ha, I thought. So that was it.

"The basic effects are there, as good as ever. All they need is modernizing; we could do it easily."

Poor Max, I thought.

"We could be on top again," she said. "He could be on top again. Where he *belongs.*" Was she, in fact, sincere then? "That's what I want—for *both* of us." No way.

"Come on now, babe," Harry reassured her. He bussed her lightly on the cheek. "It's in the bag."

She managed a sound of amusement. "If you can manage this, I'll toast you with the best champagne in town."

He ran a hand down her back and across the curve of a buttock; a Kendal move if there ever was one. "Well, I might want just a little more," he said.

He had begun to kiss her when she stiffened, looking toward the desk chair. My eyeballs struggled to the task of seeing what she saw.

In pushing the chair she had caused it to stop moving when it was reversed. (Or had it been reversed when none of us was looking?)

A puff of gray-white smoke was rising from the chair now.

Cassandra jerked away from Harry, looking stricken; that's the word.

Noting her expression and the fixed direction of her gaze, he, too, looked toward the chair. (That made three of us.) They stared at it in choked silence.

At last the chair turned slowly to reveal the final principal in the murderous drama about to unfold.

My son, Maximilian Delacorte.

chapter 5

Max was still a very handsome man. His hair, though streaked with gray, was full and dark. His vandyke beard set off the perfect cut of his features. Like me, he was tall and well-proportioned, his presence something to behold. (As in all modesty I say it—mine was too.)

He wore a wine-red smoking jacket over his white shirt and four-in-hand tie. Around his neck hung a gold chain with a pair of glasses dangling from it. In the fingers of his left hand, he held the thin cigar he was smoking.

He blew out smoke and smiled at them. "Good afternoon," he said. His tone was mild. *He must not have heard them plotting,* I thought. He sounded too benign.

Cassandra and Harry could only stare (perhaps *gape* is the word) at him, so caught off guard were they. Like myself, they were clearly wondering how long he'd been sitting there and what he'd heard. Unlike me, they were (I hope) ridden with guilt and dreading that he'd heard it all.

Max looked across the room at me and signaled, smiling. "And good afternoon to you, *Padre,*" he said.

How I wished I could return his smile and signal. Lord above, how I wished I could blow the whistle on those two; those three if I included Brian with his most suspicious facsimile of Cassandra.

It now became apparent that Harry, at least, was wondering more than whether Max had heard his plot or no.

He was also wondering where in God's name Max had come from in the first place. The chair had been empty, and it stood behind the desk with no proximity to any wall Max might have popped from.

It then became evident that Cassandra was wondering the same thing.

Unlike Harry, however, she meant to use the puzzle as a means to—hopefully—gloss over what Max might have heard of their conversation—or, for that matter, seen of their physical adhesion.

She pointed at the chair. "When did you build *that?*" she asked, her tone indicating a chiding amusement she could not possibly have been experiencing.

Max smiled pleasantly. "When you were in Bermuda," he said. (Would I ever forget those three lovely weeks of her absence?)

"Well, you really caught us by surprise," she said, trying to retain that gloss of amusement in her voice.

"*Did* I?" Max sounded almost childlike in his gratification at having succeeded with the illusion. I knew the feeling of course, but I wished that he didn't feel it at that particular moment.

Cassandra made a sound of amusement again. "You've been saving that for the perfect moment, haven't you?" she accused.

"You like it?" he asked.

"*Do I like it?*" she responded scoldingly. "You know very well I like it. It's a wonderful effect."

He smiled and nodded, gratified again. "It *is*," he agreed.

Harry began to speak in an attempt to parallel Cassandra's pose that nothing was amiss. But Cassandra spoke first. "You came in through there," she said, pointing to the floor beneath the chair.

Max nodded. "Trap door—indistinguishable, of course."

"It's marvelous," she told him.

Harry broke his silence with a burst of (excessive) enthusiasm. "Marvelous?" he cried. "It's *dynamite!* Hey, Max!"

He moved behind the desk, where Max stood to greet him. Was I the only one to note how labored Max's movements were? No, at least one other person noted it as well.

Max took Harry's thrust-out hand in both of his.

"How *are* you, pal?" asked Harry.

"Very well, old friend," Max answered. "And you?"

"Not complaining," Harry replied.

Max smiled at him; a tired smile, I thought. "You've been lying in the sun," he said.

"You know me, Max," said Harry with a grin. "A little sun, a little run. Keeps the blood in motion."

Max reached up to touch Harry's hair. "Plugs flourishing, I see," he teased.

Harry chuckled, obviously not pleased to have his implants mentioned. I wished I could have laughed aloud. I hadn't known about them.

"Not bad, anh?" said Harry, pretending that he wasn't displeased.

At which point in the procedure, who should stride into the room but Brian? As himself now naturally, hair dark, male clothes, his resemblance to Cassandra nonetheless apparent. "Hi," he said to Harry, smiling.

"How you doin', kid?" Harry responded. He extended his right hand and Brian squeezed it in momentary greeting.

"Fine," said Brian. "How are you?"

"Couldn't be better," Harry said.

"Good," said Brian.

Their politesse was total sham. Harry had nothing but contempt for Brian, whom he regarded as a no-talent leech, a gofer to the bone. Brian, in turn, loathed Harry for a number of reasons which will presently emerge; I have to follow the rules of proper story-telling, don't I?

At any rate, they smiled and spoke most pleasantly to one another. Absolute hypocrisy.

It was going to be that kind of day.

Brian removed a slip of paper from his shirt pocket and handed it to Max. "Everything you want on here?" he asked. *Everything I have to go-fer?* I added in my mind.

Max put his glasses on and perused the list. He nodded. "I believe so. Aren't you a little late departing, though?"

Brian shook his head. "Train doesn't leave for thirty minutes."

"You off?" asked Harry, totally disinterested, I knew, but maintaining his pose of sociability—an agent's skill.

"Have to pick up props in Boston," Brian told him.

"Ah-ha." Harry nodded. "Have a good trip, then."

Brian nodded. "Thank you." He turned to Cassandra. "We'd better go," he said.

"Be right with you," she replied. "Wait in the car."

"All right." Once more, Brian smiled at Harry. "Nice to see you again," he said.

"The same," said Harry, reciprocating the lie.

"See you later, Max," Brian said.

Max did not reply but raised one languid hand. I didn't really know what he thought of Brian. I had always assumed that, however kindly disposed he might be to his young brother-in-law, he could not have had too much respect for him. How little respect I found out later.

Brian walked to the doorway and exited into the entry hall.

As he did, Cassandra turned to Max with a look of grave concern. "Harry told me you asked him to come here," she said. "I hope—"

She broke off, sighing. "Well, you know what I hope," she added.

Moving to Max, she kissed him on the left cheek, then regarded him anxiously. "It can all be what it was," she said.

Max smiled at her. "Let's see what happens," he told her.

Never had a harrowing event-to-be been heralded with such offhandedness.

Cassandra looked at him as though she hoped to penetrate his eyes and see into his very thoughts. Then, with an evanescent smile, she turned toward the doorway. "See you in a little while," she said. She glanced at Harry. "I've driving Brian to the station," she explained.

"Good." He nodded. "Give the boss and me a chance to talk."

Another fleeting smile from her. "Will you still be here when I get back?" she asked.

"How long?" he responded.

"Less than an hour."

"I imagine so," said Harry. "Though I *do* have to get back to Boston by early evening." (The well-laid plans . . .)

Cassandra nodded and left, closing the door, Harry and Max watching her departure.

After she was gone, Harry smiled at Max. "Quite a gal you've got there," he said.

"Quite a gal," repeated Max. For several seconds he looked at Harry, face expressionless. *What is he thinking?* I wondered.

Then he smiled. "Well, old friend," he said, "I thank you for coming."

"My pleasure, pal," Harry replied expansively.

Max gestured toward the chairs. "Shall we?" he inquired.

Harry's smile was wry; at least, he thought it was. "That's what I'm here for," he responded.

He moved to the chair, where he had set down his attaché case and hat, which he picked up and placed on the table.

In the meantime, Max had headed for the bar. Glancing over, Harry noticed (as I did, worriedly) his sluggish gait and grimaced to himself.

"Your usual Scotch?" asked Max.

"No, no, just a diet soda if you have it," Harry answered. "Too early for the hard stuff."

Max peered beneath the bar and came up with a can of Diet Coke. "Are you hungry?" he asked.

Harry shook his head. "No. Had my little health-food breakfast before I left Boston."

Max pulled the can tab free and asked, "Why Boston?" He picked up the silver tongs to put ice cubes in a glass.

"Opening tonight," said Harry. "Client of mine."

"Sounds exciting," commented Max.

"It is—for him," said Harry. "His first play. A murder mystery."

"Never can believe them," Max replied; it was a remark immersed in irony, considering what was about to happen.

"Neither can I," fawned Harry. "But the public likes 'em if they're well done. This one is."

"Glad to hear it," Max responded, starting over with the glass of Diet Coke on ice cubes. Harry hesitated, then apparently felt compelled to say, "You're movin' kind o' slow, pal."

"Am I?" Max reached the chairs and handed the drink to Harry.

"Thanks, Max," Harry murmured, watching Max settle into the other chair with a faint, but unmistakably weary, groan. *What's going on?* I thought; *I've never seen him look so bad.*

Harry winced at the sight but managed a smile as Max looked over at him. He held the glass up toastingly. "To the best," he said.

Max appeared amused as Harry took a sip of Diet Coke, then set the glass down on the table. Max lifted a cigar box from the table and raised its lid, holding it out to Harry, who gestured *no*. "That stuff'll kill you," he remarked; another inadvertently ironic statement.

"The least of my problems at the moment," Max replied.

His voice sounded so tired that Harry nearly commented on it, I noted. Then, changing direction, Harry gestured toward the casket, grinning. "Love that figure in there," he said. "A new gimmick maybe?"

Max shook his head. "Just wanted to see what I'd look like."

"*Jesus Christ.*" Harry made a face. "Cassandra told me that, but I couldn't really believe her."

"Why not?" asked Max in mild surprise.

Harry looked askance at him. "*Max,*" he said.

"My future home inside my present one," Max said. "Seems logical to me."

"Come on." Clearly, Harry still had trouble believing it; but then, he was unable to approach the thinking of a Delacorte.

Max smiled tiredly, flexing his fingers with effort, wincing as he did. Again I noted Harry on the verge of saying something, then discarding the idea. He took another sip of Diet Coke and set the glass back down. "All right," he said. "Shall we get on with it?"

The lid of Pandora's box was about to be raised.

chapter 6

No, wait. Before we do," said Harry. I saw him brace himself. "You know Cassandra's really worried about you."

"She's said so," Max acknowledged.

"*Said* so?" Harry frowned. "You don't believe her?"

Max did not reply. Stubbing out his cigar on an ashtray,
he reached down beside himself on the chair and picked up
a red billiard ball; I hadn't noticed it there. (Well, my obser-
vation powers weren't *perfect*, you know, as you will see.)

Tossing the ball into his left hand, he dropped it back into
his right.

"Max, you know she's on your side," said Harry.

Max did not respond. Again, he tossed the ball into his
left hand, letting it drop to his right once more.

A third time, he made the tossing motion, but the ball
now disappeared. (Palmed in his right, of course, the elementary *Throw Vanish*.)

"Max, she wants the best for you," Harry told him.

His features hardened as Max continued playing with the
billiard ball, causing it to Reproduce, then Reproduce again,

his face intent as he performed "Twirls" with his thumb and forefinger to prove that what was actually a shell was another solid billiard ball.

An attempted "Acquitment" (transfer of the ball from right to left hand) to create another "Vanish" failed, and the billiard ball fell to his lap. Angrily, he picked it up again.

"Max, come *on*," said Harry, trying to sound patient—in vain.

Max said nothing but began again, the billiard ball becoming two, then three. He waved his right hand up and down, the ball between his first and middle fingers "hinged back" into the shell. *Now you've got it, Sonny boy*, I thought.

At which, he dropped the ball again. It bounced off his lap to hit the carpeting and roll away. Max slumped back and closed his eyes. "Ta*da*," he muttered, a forlorn fanfare to his faltering hands. (I felt his despair; only another magician could truly say that.)

"Let it go, pal," Harry told him, revealing unmistakably with those words that he could not possibly understand. "We have Vegas to discuss." He was unable to conceal the edge of irritation in his voice.

Max opened his eyes. "Yes," he agreed. "We have Vegas to discuss."

———

Rising from his chair, Harry retrieved the fallen billiard ball and set it on the table. Then, reseating himself, he opened his attaché case and removed two copies of a contract, handing one to Max, who put on his glasses to read it.

Noticing the lenses, Harry asked, "A little *thick*, aren't they?"

"One step removed from a Seeing Eye dog," Max answered.

Harry did not attempt to conceal his grimace. "Can't you get contacts or something?"

"Hadn't thought about it," Max replied.

"Well, *think* about it," Harry said. "I have another client who had bad eyesight, cataracts. Implants gave him back his vision better than it ever was." Another grimace. "How long has this been going on?"

"Some little time now."

Harry whistled softly. "That's no good, Max. Have you seen a doctor?" Since he already knew the answer to that, I presumed he wanted to hear Max's version of the situation.

"What for?" Max responded. "I know what the diagnosis would be. 'You're going blind, Mr. Delacorte.' Who needs to hear it?"

"*Blind*, Max?" Harry stared at him, appalled; but not half as much as I was. When had all *this* started?

"Well, not quite," Max said. "It's coming, though."

Harry swallowed, looking at his client, not his friend, I know. As it turned out, he was doubtless wondering if his visit and intended conversation were pointless now.

He drew in a straining breath then. Oh, well, he thought (my guess). May as well go on with it. If it turns out to be pointless, let it happen when I'm somewhere else. I think I read his mind correctly. One-dimensional at best, connected directly to his facial muscles.

"Okay," he said. "Let's move on."

Max cupped a hand behind his left ear. "Pardon?"

Harry stared at him, expression pained. (It looked pained, anyway.) *"Your hearing, too?"* he asked.

Max didn't answer.

"Have you tried a hearing aid?" asked Harry.

Max shook his head.

"Have you *considered* trying a hearing aid?" Harry persisted.

"I've considered everything," Max said. "Including suicide."

Oh, Sonny, no! my mind cried out. I would have wept if tears could flow.

Harry had twitched at Max's words. *"Hey. Max,"* he said. "I don't want to hear you talk like that." (*He* didn't want to hear it!)

Max said nothing, looking at the contract.

Harry swallowed, took a sip of Diet Coke, paused, then went on. "About the act itself," he said. Back to business; that was Harry.

Max directed a warning look at him.

"Max, *it's got to be discussed,"* said Harry. "You're playing a game with yourself by ignoring it."

Max started to speak but, sensing a power position, Harry cut him off. *"Look,"* he said, "you're a performer in the grand tradition." He knew about grand tradition? What a shock. "You always have been. No one's ever going to take that from you. You made magic into an art form."

"My *father* made it into an art form," Max corrected him. "I merely sustained the tradition." *God bless you for that, Son.*

"Whatever," Harry said, disinterested. "That's not the point. The point is, you're closing your mind to the facts of life.

"It's not nineteen-thirty anymore—or the forties or the fifties; *or* the sixties. What was good enough for your father and you doesn't cut it anymore. By the way, does he have to be in here?"

"Yes," said Max. "It's his favorite room. Are you concerned about what he might hear?"

"What's that supposed to mean?" demanded Harry.

"Nothing," Max said. *Something,* I thought. "Go on."

Harry bared his teeth, then continued. "It's *nineteen-eighty,* pal. Las Vegas. Lake Tahoe. Reno. Theaters in places that were the *sticks* when you started out. Television. Cable. Pay-per-view. Video cassettes.

"Look at Henning; Copperfield. Everything they do is

now, Max! *Now!* Quick. Smart. Vivid. State of the art. It's no accident they're where they are. It's not the effects. It's *not!* Your effects are *still* the best. But what you're *doing* with them is behind the times, passé. You aren't up to date, you're *out of touch.* Can't you *see* that? Cassandra can."

Max stiffened noticeably at that, but Harry, sensing his position strengthening, pressed on.

"*She knows what's going on*, Max," he said. "Let her help you."

He braced himself; that was easy to see. "Especially now that your health is . . . giving you problems." I'm sure he was about to use the word "failing," then didn't have the guts.

Even so, I saw the skin drawn tight across Max's cheeks.

"All right, I shouldn't have said that," Harry retreated.

"But you did," said Max.

Harry's features tightened then. "Yes, I did," he said. "It's *said*. And—" He gritted his teeth. "Well, damn it, it's the truth, isn't it?"

Max said nothing, gazing at his agent with unblinking eyes, intimidating him.

"All right," Harry said. "I'm sorry. Shall we forge on?"

He flipped over the first page of the contract. "You're in luck," he said. "The casino still wants you. Which, under the circumstances . . ." He let the sentence hang.

"Baltimore?" asked Max.

Harry's gesture said, What else? (*My God, how bad had it been?* I wondered.)

"Word travels quickly," Max observed.

"As quickly as a phone call," Harry said. He flipped more contract pages. "The figures are on page six. And, I might add, lots more bucks than they cared to be parted from."

Max only stared at him.

Harry was about to go on when he heard the same faint

sound that I did and looked around. "What's that?" he muttered.

Max cupped a hand behind his right ear. "Pardon?"

"I-heard-a-noise," Harry said, exaggerating his pronunciation.

Max gestured vaguely. "I didn't hear anything," he said. (If he hadn't, he really *was* going deaf; I'd heard it clearly.)

Harry nodded disgruntledly. "Okay." He looked back at the contracts. "Never mind. You on page six?"

"Page six," Max said.

"You see what it is then," Harry told him. "Ten weeks. Two shows a night. Seventeen-fifty per. You understand the conditions?"

Max remained silent, and I saw how Harry tensed. Max always could get on his nerves—those gray-blue eyes, the autocratic demeanor; like father, like son.

"Do - you - understand - the - conditions?" Harry asked, once more verbally exaggerating.

When Max still didn't reply, Harry continued quickly, curtly. "Co-billing for Cassandra. Your policy regarding partial nudity to be dismissed. I'm talking topless at the very least. Not Cassandra, of course." His smile was perfunctory.

They gazed at one another and, like Harry, I began to wonder what my son was thinking; his expression was unrevealing, a face carved from stone.

"*Well?*" asked Harry.

As though in response to his words, the sound occurred again, not faintly this time. Very distinct. A *chuckle.*

Coming from the direction of the globe.

Harry scowled. "That I know you heard," he said. "I know you made it happen, too."

The smile on Max's lips was somewhat more guarded than that of the Mona Lisa.

Harry stood and moved toward the globe. Max rose to

follow. "Its a new illusion," he said. "I'm not prepared to show it yet."

"You shouldn't have used it on me, then," said Harry with a tight smile.

"You may not like it," Max warned.

"I'll take the chance," said Harry.

Reaching the globe, he examined it, finding no special feature.

He ran his hand across the curved surface.

Then he jerked it back abruptly as the outer layer of the globe rolled downward, revealing a glass globe underneath. I reacted with surprise; to what extent I could.

Harry positively twitched, so startled was he by the sight that he could not prevent a gasp from pulling back his lips.

Inside the globe was a head.

His.

chapter 7

Harry gasped at the head. There was no denying it was his. It looked real in every way.

Its eyes were closed.

"Jesus H. Christ," said Harry. Bending over, he took a closer look.

The head was larger than lifesize, I now saw. Still, it looked completely real. *When did Max do this?* I wondered. It had to have been at night when I was sleeping; when everyone was sleeping.

"What the *hell*—" muttered Harry.

He twitched again, shuddering this time and jerking erect.

The eyes of the head had opened and were looking up at him.

"*Holy Jesus,*" Harry muttered.

Then a grin of pleasure creased his face and he turned to Max.

"You son of a bitch," he said in delight. "You tricky son of a bitch."

"You like it?" Max inquired.

"Like it? *Love* it!" Harry exploded. He squinted at the head. "But what the hell *is* it?" he asked.

"Laser-produced, holographically processed, stored imagery," Max answered.

Harry gave him a hooded look. "Yeah, that's what I thought it was," he said. He peered at the head, which peered back. (Two Harry Kendals in the same room; a true example of superfluity.) "A Three-D movie, right?" he asked.

Max repressed a smile. "A bit more involved than that," he said. I felt awed pride in him. He'd carried magic into the technological age, God bless him.

"Controlled by—" Harry regarded him questioningly.

Max removed a small remote-control box from the left-hand pocket of his smoking jacket and held it up. Harry beamed. *"You son of a bitch,"* he said fondly.

He tapped the globe. "Now that's what I've been talking about," he said. "This is *today."*

"Indeed it is," said Max, meaning something other than Harry did (we soon discovered).

Harry was enthusing now. "Audiences are going to *love* it, pal! It's state of the art! Las Vegas will—"

"Forget it, Harry," interrupted Harry's head. "Las Vegas is out. Max didn't ask you here to talk about Las Vegas."

Harry and I were both astonished, staring at the head. He began to laugh, then stopped as the words he'd just heard registered.

"I don't get it," he said, the edge of irritation in his voice again.

He looked back at the head as it began to speak once more.

"Allow me to explain," it said. "The Great Delacorte has been a star for almost twenty years—as his father was before him. The Great Delacorte springs from a half-century

tradition of art and craft. Like his father, The Great Delacorte has been honored before crowned heads of Europe.

"Yet you ask him now to entertain a herd of sheep. A
gathering of dolts whose greatest passion lies in feeding
coins to slot machines. The Great Delacorte has been ac-
claimed. Respected. Celebrated. World renowned."

The voice of the head was venomous now, charged with
hatred.

"Did you really think," it said, "that The Great Delacorte
would display his wonders *on the bottom of an ornamented
garbage can?*"

It may have been my most frustrating moment in those
fourteen years—a desperate yearning to applaud with
hands that lay like sides of beef on my lap.

Harry had been stunned into silence; even anger was un-
available to him, he was so shocked.

Then anger started rising.

"Did you ask—" He broke off, furious; he had begun to
ask a question of the head.

Turning sharply to Max, he demanded, "Did you ask me
all the way up here to have this *goddam gizmo* tell me off?"

"In part," said Max.

The answer drifted over Harry's head as he stormed on.
"You knew before I came that you were going to say no,
didn't you?"

Max didn't answer. He depressed a button on the remote
control and the outer layer of the globe glided back into
place. Max returned the box to his pocket.

Harry was in a rage now. "You had no intention of taking
the Vegas job!" he railed. "Of letting Cassandra even try to
help you, much less share co-billing! Or of improving your
goddam act one goddam little bit!"

With a grimace of disgust, he turned abruptly for the
table by the chair. "Thanks to you, I've got a nice long, time-
wasting ride back to Boston now," he snarled.

"What you, euphemistically, refer to as 'the Vegas job' consists of second billing in a downtown burlesque show," said Max.

"We take what we can get, babe," Harry muttered, starting to return the contracts to his attaché case.

"Like *Magic Max*, the half-wit host on the TV kiddie show?" Max asked. (That would have made me groan if I could have; I'd never heard about it.)

"It was good money," Harry snapped. "If you had any brains, you'd have grabbed it."

"Like 'Delacorte's Dandy Magic Kit' for preschool toddlers?" Max responded.

"*It was good money, pal.*" (*Dear God*, hit *him, Max!* my brain cried.)

Harry slammed shut his attaché case, then tossed it on the chair, turning to confront Max.

"I've got news for you," he said. (The man actually *sneered* as he spoke.) "Maybe you haven't figured it out yet, but The Great Delacorte has *had* it. In touch with the fucking mysterious has had it. People wanna *laugh* today. Have fun. Be entertained."

"*Yucks?*" asked Max.

"You got it."

"*Shtick?*"

"Right on."

"*Razzmatazz?*"

"Now you're talking." Harry was still sneering.

"How about changing the name of the act to *Necromancy and Knockers?*" Max suggested. "*Bewitchment and Boobs? In Touch with the Mammaries?*"

"*Right!*" Harry shouted.

"Wrong!" Max shouted back.

"Well, set me straight, O Great and Glorious Delacorte," Harry derided.

Max had to smile at Harry's words. "That, I fear, would take an act of God," he said.

Harry made a contemptuous sound and started for the desk. Max moved to block his way—with an energy unexpected by me as well as by Harry. "Listen to me!" he said.

Harry looked at him suspiciously but wouldn't stop to listen; he started to move by Max, who clamped a hand on his arm with a grip so strong it made Harry wince. *"Listen to me, I said,"* Max told him.

"I thought you were sick," Harry said.

"That is the effect I have created, yes," Max responded. (My attention, now, was *really* caught.)

Harry's eyes had narrowed. *"What?"* he said.

"Here is the reality," Max went on, pointing at Harry. "I have no intention of degenerating with the marketplace. I will not 'do' downtown Vegas, playing a buffoon in a breakaway tuxedo while surrounding chorus girls display their silicone-enhanced protuberances.

"Neither will I 'do' moronic kiddie shows on television. I will not create and market magic kits for second-graders. I will not perform at fairs or conventions or the openings of supermarkets. I will not 'do' witless commercials.

"In brief, I will not despoil an act which I have nurtured carefully for fourteen years—which my *father* nurtured for *fifty* years. Failing eyesight, hearing on the wane, dexterity declining, I am still The Great Delacorte *and I will not dishonor that most honorable of names!"*

I felt a double-edged reaction in my vitals.

On the one hand, I felt utter agony that Max had been confronted by such humiliating offers.

On the other hand, I felt utter pride in his response to them, more pride than I had ever felt for him before.

Harry, needless to say, felt neither emotion—if he felt emotion at all, which I doubt. He gazed at Max with a baleful expression. *"Sorry,"* he said. "I thought you needed money. My mistake."

He started by Max, who grabbed his arm again, restraining him.

"If I wanted money," Max informed him, "I'd sell my blood. My *soul* is not for sale."

Bravo, Sonny! If only I could have shouted it aloud.

Harry regarded Max with cold amusement. "Big words, my friend," he said.

Pulling loose, he walked around Max and headed for the desk again.

"True words," Max told him. "And you are certainly not my friend. Not anymore."

"You're breaking my heart," said Harry.

Reaching the desk, he picked up the telephone and punched out a number, placing the receiver to his ear.

Max followed him. Among the items on his desk was a long Arabian dagger in an ivory sheath. Max picked it up.

"Do you have any notion whatsoever how demanding it can be to function as a stage illusionist?" he asked.

Harry ignored him but I paid close attention, feeling a warmth of nostalgic pleasure. These were words I'd spoken to Max many times in the past.

Harry spoke into the mouthpiece. "This is Kendal," he said. "Put Linda on."

"A skilled illusionist must also be a skilled actor," Max continued.

"Linda? Harry," he told his secretary. "Call Resnick and tell him that I'm on my way back to Boston; I'll probably be late."

"The actor makes us look at something, the magician makes us *not* look," Max told him at the same time.

"Yeah, right; okay," Harry said into the telephone. "Call him now."

He put down the receiver and gazed apathetically at Max, who was saying, "Two sides of the same coin. The illusion of reality versus the reality of illusion. The magic of drama versus the drama of magic." (He remembered every word, bless him.)

Harry's cheeks puffed out as he exhaled, a look of boredom on his face. He started back toward the chair on which his attaché case was lying.

"Do you know how I became The Great Delacorte?" Max asked, following again. Harry didn't even look at him. "I wasn't *born* The Great Delacorte, you know," Max continued. "I had to work to perfect the character. Just as my father had to—"

"Well, it's the *wrong character*, old boy!" Harry cut him off, pointing an accusing finger at him. "That highfalutin' bullshit may have been hot stuff when Roosevelt was in the White House, but it doesn't sell a nickel's worth today! You need something *different* now! Something—"

He broke off in disgust and moved to the chair. "You don't want to listen to advice. You know it all," he said.

Picking up his attaché case, he opened it and searched inside.

"Sit down, Harry," Max told him.

"I don't have *time* to sit down, *pal*," said Harry, his face distorted by animosity, then by fury. "Where in the fucking hell is the fucking number of that fucking cab company?" he raged.

"*Sit down*, Harry," Max repeated.

"*I don't have time—*"

His voice stopped as he heard the (chilling) sound of the dagger blade being snatched from its sheath.

Heavy silence. Harry stared at Max incredulously. (So did I.)

"Are you *threatening* me?" Harry finally asked.

Max did not reply. The dagger, pointed upward in his right hand, lowered.

Thinking he had won the point, Harry checked his gold-banded Rolex. "All right," he said. "You have five minutes, and get rid of that fucking knife."

"Dagger," Max corrected.

And he jerked his right arm up as though to hurl it straight at Harry's chest.

chapter 8

Hey!" cried Harry, alarmed and angry at the same time.

Several moments more of threat, Max's gray-blue eyes unblinking as he looked at Harry.

"Hey!" said Harry again, thoroughly intimidated.

Max stared at him.

Then, turning, he hurled the dagger at the lobby display. Harry (and I, it felt like) jolted as the blade pierced the figure of The Great Delacorte.

"How appropriate," Max observed. "Right through the heart."

A rumble of distant thunder made Harry shudder—as though the gods had just declared their displeasure.

Max and Harry stared at one another. Finally, Harry found his (labored) voice. "You're crazy, Max," he said. "You know that?"

"There *is* that possibility," Max answered calmly. "Madness is afoot in this house. Don't you feel it?" I saw that his smile was unnerving to Harry. "The very air tingles with it."

He was right; it did.

Max turned abruptly for the fireplace. "And now," he said, "sit down."

"Max, I have to *go*," said Harry. His tone was not aggressive anymore, but mollifying.

Moving swiftly, Max took down the pair of dueling pistols, put one on the desk and, carrying the other, returned to Harry, who watched him in uneasy silence. "What are you doing?" Harry murmured.

Max cupped his right hand behind his ear. "Pardon?"

"*What are you doing?*" Harry repeated.

"I loaded them this morning," Max replied, his answer an apparent non sequitur.

"What?" asked Harry.

"I said—"

"I heard what you said," Harry interrupted. "What do you mean, you *loaded* them?"

Max extended the pistol with his right hand, pointing it at Harry's heart. "I loaded them for use," he said. "Now will you kindly sit down?"

"You can't be serious about this," Harry protested. But neither he nor I had any doubt regarding Max's seriousness.

Which was proven as Max extended his arm all the way, the dark eye of the barrel quite close to Harry's chest now.

With a swallow dry enough for me to hear across the room, Harry sat down in the chair, placing his hat and attaché case back on the table.

"Do you really want your father here?" he asked, his tone weak.

"Oh, yes, definitely," Max replied. "I want him to hear it all. I only hope to God that, somewhere in his brain, he's capable of understanding and appreciating what I'm doing."

Oh, Sonny, Sonny, yes I am. My brain the only part of me that really functioned then.

"Look, I don't know what the hell you *are* doing here," said Harry nervously, "but let's not be impulsive. Let's talk about this. I think you need help, pal."

"The kind of help I got in Chicago?" Max asked softly.

Harry's face went blank.

"The kind of help I got in Des Moines?" asked Max. "In New Orleans? In Tampa?"

"What are you—"

"It took a little research on the last three," Max cut him off. "But Chicago dropped right on me in the middle of an afternoon this May. A phone call from a Mr. Charlie Haines—"

"Wait a second," Harry said.

"—inquiring why you'd turned down his generous offer; was I *sick* or something?" Max was glaring at Harry now, the pistol aimed at his head. *This is* true? I thought.

"Max, put that down," said Harry, trying in vain to sound authoritative.

"Is that the kind of help I need?" asked Max.

"Max, I only did it to *help*," Harry said. *My God, it is true,* I thought.

"Curious help—*pal*," responded Max. "Rejecting four well-paying engagements without consulting me."

"All right, I was wrong—"

His voice broke into a gasp of horror as Max abruptly jammed the barrel against his forehead. "Yes, indeed you were," said Max. "The question is, old friend . . . *why?*"

Harry tried to take in breath. He wasn't too successful at it, and his voice wheezed as he replied, "Is the answer worth killing me for?"

Max said, "Absolutely."

With his left hand, he drew back the pistol hammer.

Harry hissed, completely terrified, and closed his eyes, his face a mask entitled *Total Dread*.

When nothing happened, he opened his eyes and peered

up at my son, who towered over him, looking down with godlike disdain.

Words tumbled from Harry's mouth as he said, "I thought it would make you realize sooner that you needed help, real help. I wasn't trying to hurt you!"

He positively whined as Max pressed the barrel end tighter against his forehead. *Good,* I thought.

"Is that why you let that man look through my devices while I was on stage that night in Philadelphia?" Max asked.

"What?" asked Harry. *What?* asked my mind.

Harry groaned as Max pushed the pistol even harder against his skull.

"All right, all right," said Harry, his voice thin and shaking. "I was trying to get you some *money.*"

"By letting that man steal my magic?" said Max. *Oh, blow his goddam brains out, Sonny!* I thought.

Harry's lips were trembling. Swallowing again, he managed, "Nothing happened, Max."

"Nothing happened because it's not that easy to steal Delacorte magic." (I'd seen to that.) His voice grew hard. "But you were going to take a crack at it, weren't you?"

His finger tightened on the trigger. Harry whimpered, his eyes shutting once again. *"Dear God,"* he whispered.

Well, maybe this is not too good an idea after all, I thought.

———

Nothing happened.

Harry opened his eyes a crack to peer up at Max.

He reacted. I reacted.

Max was smiling.

"How tempting," he said, "to pull the trigger and observe your brains go flying. Every black, dismal shred of them."

Another sound of dread from Harry, followed by a sound of scoffing from my son.

"Everyone talks about how tough you are," he said. "Toughest agent in the business, Harry Kendal. Made of tempered steel."

He snickered. "Made of *cottage cheese*," he said. "Tough at selling clients down the river, yes. At life, however—?"

He chuckled and shook his head. "—a total wimp."

He turned and walked away, headed toward the desk. I must admit I felt a great relief. Whatever Harry had done—and it must have been a lot—I didn't want to see my son a murderer.

Obviously, he didn't want it either.

"What a blithering idiot you are," he said, tossing the pistol onto the desk. "To even think that a man of my degree would be capable of such barbaric murder. And in front of my *father!*" His words shamed my original urge that he do just that.

Harry watched him blankly, wondering what Max was planning next. I confess that I wondered, too.

The answer was immediate in coming as my son pulled out the top middle drawer of the desk and removed a vial.

Holding it up for Harry to see, he set it down and lifted the silver thermos decanter, pulled off its top and poured water into a glass. Putting down the decanter, he unscrewed the cover from the vial and shook four red capsules into his palms. *Oh, now what, Sonny?* I thought uneasily.

Max tossed the capsules into his mouth and, with the water, swallowed them.

"There," he said, "that should do it. Give me five minutes. Maybe ten."

Son! My mental voice was anguished.

Harry was still numbed by fright. He stared at Max uncomprehendingly.

"What are you doing?" he muttered.

The hand behind the ear. Max inquired, "Pardon?"

"What are you doing?" Harry asked again, more loudly now.

"Past tense, old friend," Max answered. "What you should say is, what have I *done?*"

Harry still didn't understand. I understood only too well.

Max tossed the empty vial to Harry—who tried to catch it, but missed; it fell into his lap. He picked it up and studied it. There was no label. He looked back at Max in confusion. Then he smelled the opening of the vial, wincing at the odor.

"Bitter almonds," Max informed him.

Arsenic, I thought in horror.

"Arsenic," said Max.

"Oh, my God." Harry labored to his feet. "You're *crazy.*"

"I believe we've already established that," said Max.

Harry rushed to the desk, his legs appearing somewhat rubbery. He snatched up the telephone receiver.

"A waste of time," Max told him calmly. I felt ill. "I'll be dead long before anyone can get here."

Harry looked at him in agitation. "What the hell do you expect me to do, just stand by and watch you die?" he demanded.

Why not? My thought was stricken. *It's all I can do. Except that I'll be sitting by instead.*

"Just stand by," said Max, "and offer me the courtesy of listening with attention for the last few minutes of my life."

"Oh, God," said Harry—and my mind—and stared at Max.

Then he said, impulsively, "I'll drive you to the hospital in your car!"

"There isn't time," Max told him quietly. The calmness of his tone was chilling to my blood. "I have five to seven minutes left at most. Sit down."

"Jesus, Max!"

"*Sit down,*" said Max. His smile was thin. "And, for once in your life, *listen* to me."

"*Jesus,*" Harry mumbled.

There's nothing I can do to stop this. There was utter, helpless horror in my mind. *Nothing!*

Harry didn't sit; he couldn't. (I could do nothing but.) He watched Max with a pained expression as my son began to pace around the room.

"The more I get my circulation going, the less time it will take," he said.

"*Jesus, Max!*"

Max raised a silencing hand.

"I never told you about Adelaide, did I?" he asked. "My true love. My only love. My wife. My friend. My treasure."

Not that, my mind pleaded. Adelaide had always been an angel to me.

"I was married to her before you came along," continued Max. "Before Cassandra came along."

Harry twitched (I may have done the same without sensation) as Max's right leg seemed to buckle momentarily and he staggered slightly. Harry made a sudden move toward him, then stopped as Max walked on, a look of haunted recollection on his face.

"Those were the best years of my life," he said. "We loved each other deeply. I was happier than I have ever been."

I closed my eyes and prayed to weep. I always knew that Max adored her; I could see it in his every word and action, in his face. My son adored her as I'd adored my wife, and both of us had lost those magic, wonderful relationships.

Max started to go on and, for several seconds, his voice grew thick. I saw him struggle to prevent its happening again before he'd finished what he had to say.

"My joy was her beside me," he continued, pacing once again. "Her love unquestioning. I idolized her, Harry. I'm sure you think that such an emotion was never possible for me. *He* knew though," he added, pointing at me. "He saw it all."

I did, my son, I thought, agonized, opening my eyes again.

"She was, to me, everything that was good. Everything that was pure and beautiful and innocent."

His last word was emphasized involuntarily, accompanied by a wince of pain. Harry went stiff with apprehension.

For several moments, Max stood motionless, eyes hooded, breathing slowly.

"Max, let me call an ambulance, for God's sake!" Harry cried.

Max waved him off and started pacing once again, his movements uneven now.

"She was carrying our child when the accident occurred," he said, his voice tormented. I wished, in vain of course, that I could, by closing my eyes, shut away the entire scene.

"She was tired," Max said. "I insisted that she stay at home. She wouldn't hear of it. She had to be on stage with me. Helping me. Supporting me.

For God's sake, stop the self-torture! I thought.

Max stopped and leaned against the frame of the picture window, breath erratic as he looked out toward the gazebo. "Getting dark," he said. "A storm is coming."

He turned from the window, his expression rigid as though to hold away the pain.

"It was too much for her," he said, beginning to pace again, weaving now. (I stared at him in anguish.) "She misjudged. She didn't move quite fast enough. A piece of heavy equipment fell."

He stopped, throwing a hand across his eyes as though to blot away the memory of that hideous night.

"My wife," he murmured brokenly. "Our child." He threw back his head. "All in one dread moment!"

He clenched his teeth, pushing his left hand to his stomach.

"*Max,*" said Harry.

Max paid no attention to him. Hand pressed hard against his stomach, features set in a grimace of pain, he began to pace again. *I can't bear this,* I thought.

"She's been dead for twelve years now," he said. "Yet still I love her—only her. My darling and my angel. There's never been another like her. There never could be; *never.*"

With a breathless cry of pain, he fell toward one of the chairs, hands shooting down to brake himself on the chair back.

He struggled to a standing position as Harry ran over, a look of hapless dread on his face. Max reached out a trembling hand to pat him weakly on the arm.

"This is the best way out . . . old friend," he mumbled, sounding very weak. *It's not the best way out for me,* my mind screamed, half in terror, half in rage.

"It's not only Adelaide who's gone," Max continued. He drew in a straining breath. "Everything is gone—you know that as well as I."

I'm not gone! I thought. *I may be useless, but I'm still around!*

Max groaned and clenched his teeth again, hand pressed to his stomach. "God," he murmured.

He forced a smile; there was no amusement in it. "Yes, everything is gone," he said. "My hands, my eyes, my ears, my marriage, my career." He paused. "And now my life," he finished.

I'm *not gone, Sonny,* my thought, admittedly, one of wretchedness.

With a brief, hollow cry, Max dropped to his knees beside the chair, twisting in a paroxysm of pain, eyes staring, face a mask of agony.

Harry managed to help him into the chair, and Max slumped back, his breathing labored. "God," he said again. He began to gag, unable to breath. His mouth opened, and his tongue lolled out for several moments.

Then, with a wheezing moan, his body convulsed, jerked a few times, and went limp, his eyes falling shut.

chapter 9

I felt my heartbeat thudding heavily, an old drum in the cavity of my chest, beaten with a slow and weary stroke. I wondered why it hadn't split in two.

Harry gaped in silence at my son. Finally, he spoke.

"Jesus," he said. "Oh, Jesus. Jesus H. Christ."

Bending over, he pressed his right ear to Max's chest, listening intently, trying to hold his shaking breath long enough to hear the beat of Max's heart—or, more likely, the absence of it.

Which is what he heard; nothing.

He jerked erect and looked at Max in shock.

Then—incredibly—in *fury*.

Spewing out words which, to my dying day, will typify the man for me.

"You lousy son of a bitch," he said. "Now I'll *never* get to Boston by tonight."

The shriek of horror he emitted was that of a woman as Max leaped up, eyes wide and glaring, and grabbed him by the arms.

Harry tore loose from Max's grip and, losing balance, flopped down on the carpeting.

Sprawling there, breath barely functioning, he gaped up at my son.

"*Surprise!*" said Max.

Silence then as Max walked over to my wheelchair and laid his right hand on my shoulder.

"I apologize for frightening you, *Padre,*" he said. "But I wanted you, of all people, to see the effect. It *was* a grand one, wasn't it?"

Leaning over, he kissed me on the cheek, then turned away and walked back to Harry. *Sonny, Sonny,* I was thinking, *what is happening in your mind?*

Reaching Harry, he began explaining—in a positively cheerful voice.

"Let me anticipate your questions," he said. "One, the capsules: B-complex. I added the smell of bitter almonds to fool you. Two, the lack of heartbeat as you listened: A skill I learned in India from one Pandit Khaj, a fakir of surpassing knowledge."

Pandit Khaj! Of course! I thought. *How could I have forgotten that?*

"Three, my heartrending performance," Max was saying. "Have I not told you that a magician is, first and foremost, a skilled actor?"

Skilled indeed, I thought. *Enough to almost finish me off, Sonny boy.*

Harry found his voice then.

"You bastard," he said. *"You dirty, miserable, shit-faced, mother-fucking, cocksucking son of a bitch!"*

"Kudos," Max responded. "You appear to have incorporated all the major profanities in one sentence. I shall forthwith notify *The Guinness Book of Records.*"

Ambivalence raged within me. I wanted to bop my son on the head for putting me through such an ordeal.

I also wanted to laugh aloud. (I've always yearned for the unreachable.)

Harry, on the other hand, was obviously not experiencing ambivalence at all. The emotion he felt was singular and pure.

Revulsion.

With a shake of his head, he pushed to his feet and moved unevenly to the chair. Picking up his attaché case and hat, he started for the entry hall.

Max strode quickly to the desk and reached beneath it.

As Harry approached the door, I heard a click in the latching mechanism. Harry turned the knob and tried to pull the door in. It would not move.

Harry didn't turn. I saw his face gone hard. In a low-pitched voice, trembling with anger, he said, "Unlock the door, Max."

Max did not reply. Harry waited, then spoke again, his tone more vehement. *"Unlock the door,* Max," he ordered.

No response.

Harry whirled, cheeks flushed with rage. "Unlock the fucking door!" he shouted.

Max did not reply or move.

With a teeth-clenched grimace, Harry lunged toward the desk.

Max picked up the pair of dueling pistols and stepped aside as his frothing agent searched for the button which would unlock the door.

"All right, where *is* it?" he demanded. He kept groping underneath the desk in vain. "Damn it!" he cried. He glared at Max.

Then a vengeful smile pulled back his lips. "All right," he said. "I'm calling the police."

Max shifted one of the pistols to his left hand, extending the other in his right, pointed at Harry's chest.

"I wouldn't," he said.

Harry's snarl was soundless. "Another of your frigging little tricks?"

Max's smile was barely visible.

"Care to test that supposition?" he inquired.

Harry wasn't sure anymore; Max was behaving too erratically.

He did not pick up the telephone receiver.

Still, his fury bubbled over, uncontrollable.

"You went through all that *shit* before—the arsenic, the phony death—just to get back at me?"

"In part," Max answered quietly.

"All that crap about your precious Adelaide?" Harry sneered.

Mistake.

He twitched with a grunt of shock as Max's face went rigid and his arm abruptly levered out, pointing the pistol at Harry's head.

Harry cried out in stunned dismay as Max pulled the trigger and the pistol fired with a deafening report.

On the mantelpiece, a vase exploded like a bomb, shooting terra-cotta shrapnel in all directions, making Harry gasp and fling his arms up automatically. In his agitated state, he'd failed to notice Max's wrist cock to the left an instant before he fired. I'd noticed, but it hadn't relieved my state of mind—I was still distressed (is it overly flippant to say: *to the max?*) by my son's behavior.

Harry stared at Max in total apprehension now. Max stared back with deep malevolence.

"Everything I said about my Adelaide stands uncontradicted," he said softly, vengefully. "Except for my mother and father, she was the only genuine person I ever had in my life."

Harry shuddered as Max put the fired pistol on the desk and shifted the other one to his right hand. He smiled at Harry.

It was not a reassuring smile . . . to either of us.

"I take it back," he said. "That pistol ball was also genuine. You demean me, Harry, by suggesting that I deal in nothing but 'frigging little tricks.' "

"What do you want?" asked Harry in a faint voice.

My question exactly.

"Well, I had considered a duel," said Max, "for a number of reasons. Honor. Revenge. Whatever."

His expression of regret was a mocking one.

"That's now impossible, however," he continued, "since I had to fire *your* pistol to prove that both weapons were really loaded."

His face went hard now, and he gestured toward a chair with the pistol. "*Sit*," he said.

Harry tried to tough it out; his voice was not exactly convincing as he muttered, "No."

"Very well," said Max.

He extended the pistol toward Harry.

"This time I will not destroy a vase," he said. "Farewell, old chum."

———

"All right," said Harry quickly. He hurried to the chair and sat.

"Now put down your little hand-stitched, leather, monogrammed-in-gold attaché case," Max told him.

Harry swallowed dryly, placing his attaché case and hat on the table beside him.

"Very good," said Max.

Harry drew in a shaking breath. "What the hell do you think you're doing, Max?" he asked.

"Wrapping up loose ends," Max answered. *"Pal."*

Keeping his eyes on Harry, he edged over to the desk and pulled out its middle drawer. Removing two folded sheets of paper, he unfolded one of them.

"Found in Cassandra's raincoat pocket," he explained.

Harry swallowed again. I actually heard the crackling of membranes in his parched throat. He watched uneasily as Max returned to the chair and began to read the letter he was holding in his left hand.

" '*Sometimes, I wonder why I bother anymore. God knows, he doesn't make me more than petty cash these days. He's washed up but too stubborn to admit it. If he keeps making a fool of himself on stage, I'm going to drop him from the agency or let some flunky handle him.*'

"Shall I go on?" he asked.

Harry stared up at my son, his eyes like cold stones; the look which, I am certain, paralyzed untold numbers of business contacts.

"It's a hard world, Max," he said. "Nobody's out there to do you favors."

"Dog-eat-dog, eh, Harold?" Max responded.

"You got it, pal," said Harry. Clearly, he was vowing not to let Max see any further signs of weakness in him. He gestured toward the letter with contempt.

"Is that why you're doing all this?" he asked. "Because I wrote an unflattering note?"

Unflattering? I thought. *Insulting, you bastard!*

"No, there's a bit more," Max replied.

In spite of his obvious vow, Harry could not restrain a shudder as Max shook open the second folded sheet of paper. Perhaps I shuddered, too; who knows?

"One sworn affidavit, duly notarized," he said. "Signed by one Emmanuel Farber, night porter at *The Essex House*.

"Statement: '*Yes, I saw that man*'—identifying a photograph of you, dear Harold—'*and that woman*'—identifying a photograph of guess who, Harold?—'*enter Room 525 on the night of April 28*—' "

"All right, I *fucked* her!" Harry interrupted, with desperate bravado. "*So what?* I didn't start it! *She* did! She wanted it, I gave it to her! Big deal! What do you expect? You can't even get it up anymore!"

If I had been my son and held that pistol in my hand, I would have blown out Harry's brains exactly then.

It was a compounded fury I was feeling at that loathsome toad of a man. The crimes?

One, a snarling admission that he'd gone to bed with Cassandra.

Two, a casual dismissal of the incident.

Three, a weaseling out from all responsibility. It was *her* fault, her desire, her demand. All he'd done was accommodate the bitch.

Four, the final insult, mocking my son as impotent.

Kill him, I thought.

But Max did not respond as I did. Did not raise the pistol to fire. Merely gazed at Harry in regret. (Regret!)

"The irony of ironies," he finally said, "is that I trusted you completely, considered you my friend."

"That was your mistake," said Harry. I saw him flinch as though in shock at his suicidal reply.

Still, he couldn't stop himself. "If you're looking for an apology, forget it," he added.

Madness, I thought.

I myself flinched as Max raised the pistol, aiming it between Harry's frozen eyes.

"There is only one thing I'm looking for," Max said. "That is revenge. And I am about to exact it."

chapter 10

Harry braced himself. Death was coming now. He was certain of it; I could see it in his face.

And yet, instead—maddeningly now!—Max said, "You never understood me for a moment, did you? Never understood the endless time and work I expended to perfect my skill."

What tangent now? I thought. *Is he going to shoot Harry or not?*

Harry was clearly wondering the same thing. He stared at Max uncertainly, anticipating death, yet wondering at the same time when it was due.

"I have been the best," Max was saying. "As my father was before me. The *best*.

"And *why?* Because I saw to everything. *Everything.* Consistency of attitude. Consistency of detail."

In an eerie way, it was like hearing myself speak. Max and I resembled one another. Our voices (when I had one) were alike.

And certainly the words he spoke, I had spoken—if not word for word then, surely, feeling for feeling.

"Consistency of detail," he repeated. "Speaking clearly to the last row as to the first. Speaking to my audience as though the words are coming for the first time instead of being repeated verbatim as they've been for twenty years."

Dear Lord, an echo of my own repeated declarations.

"Preparing monologues not only for the audience to hear," said Max, "but for myself to *think* as well. Soundless lines for me to think *between* the words I speak aloud. Details."

Was I smiling? Surely not; I couldn't. But inside I was. Inside I felt a warmth of sweet nostalgia.

Max had lowered the pistol now and begun to pace again. I saw Harry watch him with suspicion. And knew that he was thinking, *Now what?*—for I was thinking it as well, despite my pleasure at the words my son was speaking.

"*Details,*" Max said, gesturing with his left hand.

"You must not surprise an audience. You must 'stage-surprise' them. An audience loathes to be *truly* surprised, because it is unexpected, therefore unenjoyable."

The inner smile again. These words, like benedictions from the past. I wonder if he knew the pleasure they were giving me.

"The 'stage-surprise' is different," he continued. "Openly announced in advance. The magician declaring: 'My friends, I am going to surprise you. Are you ready? Prepare yourself carefully. Here it comes.' "

I was not a hunching cabbage in a wheelchair now, not a worthless lump of detritus. I was back in the world I knew and loved, and Max, my son, had taken me there.

"*Details,*" he said again.

"The choosing of a volunteer. One who will cooperate. Bright outfit, never drab. Eye-catching. Preferably female.

Not overly attractive, though. If she's too attractive, she'll draw excess attention from the act."

Quite so, I thought; *absolutely right.*

"If a male," said Max, "someone with a physical odd-ity—skinny, fat, protruding ears, whatever. Someone to amuse the audience. Distract it.

"And look *before the need*," he added. "Let them be al-ready chosen when the time arrives to use them."

Absolutely, I reacted.

Max was coming to life now, as I was (well, relatively)—his eyes bright, his posture alert, his voice increasingly ex-cited as he spoke; and why not? Wasn't this his kingdom?

Hadn't it been mine?

"What will these volunteers be used for?" he asked. The question was academic, of course; he already knew the an-swer. "Helpers? Subjects? Subjects must be credulous, not doubtful, not distrusting."

Harry would have made a lousy Subject, it occurred to me.

"Lenders of objects?" Max was adding further academic queries. "Watches? Keys? Pens? Lenders must be chosen for appearance of integrity. The same for inspectors of de-vices. The audience must trust their judgment."

How well I had taught him; I basked in the knowledge.

Now Harry tensed as Max moved to the desk and set the pistol down, then began to use both hands to gesture as he continued pacing. *Is that a good idea?* I fretted. What if Max moved so far from the desk that Harry could make a rush for the pistol? Surely he would do it. There was no other way out for him.

It seemed as though Harry listened now with one ear (as they say), keeping himself prepared to move should the op-portunity arise. *Watch it, Son,* I thought. *Don't get so carried away by your rhapsodizing that you overlook basic caution.*

"As for me, the magician," Max was saying; he seemed to have completely forgotten the pistol. "I must show no sign of strain or stiffness in the hands, the elbows, or the shoulders. Gestures must be practiced to perfection—even the smallest one."

He demonstrated some. "Their length," he said. "Their speed. Never more than one at a time."

Watch it, Sonny boy, I thought.

"*Time,*" said Max, so loudly that it made Harry twitch. "Pauses. Counts and rhythms. Root out everything which might distract. Useless movements. Pointless jewelry. Clothes that call attention to themselves.

"*And always an alternative ending; always,*" he said. "One must look ahead. Things can go wrong."

Yes, they can, I thought. *Like an agent rushing to a desk and snatching up a pistol.*

It disturbed me to see that Max's gaze was so inward now. I'm not sure he even knew that Harry was in the same room with him. And I saw that even wooden-witted Harry sensed this and was readying his move.

"Consider every detail," Max was saying (or was it The Great Delacorte, father and son, who spoke?). "Lighting. Music. Apparatus. Stagehands. Posture. Footwork; one kind for a cross, another for climbing steps. Another for moving upstage, yet another for moving down."

He began to demonstrate as to a class of novices. Ambivalence tore at me. I loved what he was saying but feared that, in saying it, he had become too incautious. I saw Harry edging forward on the chair. *Oh, God, to have a voice!* my mind exploded with lamenting rage.

"The eight positions of the body," Max was saying, demonstrating as he spoke. "Full back. Three-quarter right. Right profile. Quarter right. Full front. Quarter left. Left profile. Three-quarter left. Return to full back."

Harry started up, then sank down hurriedly as Max

turned back. Was it possible that Max was playing with him? If so, he was taking greater risks than were prudent.

"The six positions of the feet," Max told him, smiling as he demonstrated. (He *was* lost in his kingdom!) "Feet together, side by side, pointing forward. Either foot one step sideways so the feet are twelve to twenty-four inches apart. One foot perpendicular to the other, the heel of the perpendicular touching the arch of the other."

Despite uneasiness, I could not but be awed by the detailed lengths to which Max had gone to perfect his act. Even *I* had not gone so far, I admit (with contrition).

"The perpendicular foot one step forward," he was continuing, "one foot pointing forward, the other at a forty-five-degree angle to it, the heel of the angled foot touching the toe of the first.

"The same, but with the angled foot a step forward in the direction it points."

Look out, Max, I was thinking anxiously. Harry's arms were rigid as he pressed down on the armrests, preparing himself to lurch up. How could Max not notice?

"Never more than three steps at a time," Max was saying, transported, words falling quickly from his lips. "Quick steps. Slow. Exaggerated strides." He demonstrated each with delicate precision. "Details, always details."

Harry was leaning forward now, muscles quivering. *Any moment now,* I thought. *For God's sake, Max, wake up!*

"How to take applause," Max said. "Never beg for it, but never bully either. When to stifle it. When to encourage it. Never let it die completely as you bow."

Max, that's fascinating information, but don't you see that Harry is drawing in quick, strengthening breaths?

Apparently not. He kept on speaking, demonstrating.

"The art of taking bows. Face front for small ones. Eyes on the audience, never missing anyone."

Max! Harry's body was starting to rise.

"They will increase their applause if you look at them directly," Max said, all unaware. "Bow to the center. Bow to the left. Bow to the right."

Harry's gaze was fixed on the magician. My gaze ping-pong-balled between the two of them.

"Bow from the waist for loud applause," Max said. " 'Thank you! You are very kind!' " His eyes were positively glazed. " 'I'm very pleased to—' "

Three things happened simultaneously (four, if you count the painful leap of my heart).

Harry jumped up from the chair and started quickly for the desk.

I heard the sound of the front door closing in the entry hall.

And Max, brought back abruptly from his dreaming state, saw Harry and moved quickly to the desk, grabbing up the pistol. If I was not already slumped, I would have slumped.

Harry froze in his tracks, staring at my son.

Footsteps moved across the entry hall: the giveaway clack of a woman's heels.

Harry opened his mouth to cry out.

The sound strangled in his throat as Max extended the pistol toward him, his expression threatening.

"Damn!" whined Harry, in an agony of frustration, I believe. Should he cry out anyway? Risk being shot?

He couldn't. He was too afraid.

***

Both men stiffened (I did too, albeit unnoticeably) as the doorknob turned and someone tried to enter.

"Max?" said a voice—Cassandra.

Max did not respond, and, from his menacing look and gesture, he made it clear to Harry that he was not to speak either.

"Why is the door locked?" Cassandra asked.

No response. (Least of all from me.)

"What's going *on* in there?" Cassandra demanded, voice rising.

Max cleared his throat. His voice was calmly affable.

"Nothing's going on," he said. "Come back in a few minutes. I'll have something interesting to show you."

Moments passed. Despite his dread, Harry almost spoke. Only Max's repeated brandishing of the pistol stopped him.

"All right," said Cassandra.

Her footsteps moved away.

Max smiled (not the kind of smile I'd like directed at me). "Something interesting to show you," he repeated.

The masking smile fell away. *"Your lover's corpse,"* he finished.

He walked toward Harry, pistol still extended.

"You're not going to shoot me," Harry said with unconvincing bravado.

"I'm not?" said Max. "I don't—"

He broke off as Harry's gaze leaped to one of the other windows. My gaze did likewise; the only part of me that *could* leap. Max whirled, reacting.

Cassandra was standing at the window looking in, an expression of shock on her face.

Suddenly, she turned away and rushed out of sight. *To call the Sheriff?* I wondered. *To get a pistol she owned?*

Max turned back.

"Well, dear Harold," he said, "it's about that time."

"She'll call the police," Harry warned.

"The Sheriff," Max corrected. "But I doubt it. Why should she? Because of you? She never cared for you. You were, like me, merely a stepping-stone." His smile grew iced. "Or should I say a sleeping-stone?"

He pointed the pistol at Harry's chest.

"Max, don't do it," Harry pleaded.

The front door slammed shut loudly. Cassandra's shoe heels clacked rapidly across the entry hall. She threw herself against the door.

"Max!" she cried.

"Farewell, old friend," said Max.

He fired.

chapter 11

I would have cried out if I'd had the power. As always, however, I remained a soundless squash.

It was Harry who cried out in hoarse amazement as a gout of blood erupted from his white shirt. Stumbling back, he slipped and fell.

Cassandra screamed. *"Max!"*

She pounded on the door as Max watched Harry.

Harry was slouched on the floor, staring down at his shirtfront. He might well have been dead, he was so completely motionless.

He lived, however. Stunned and breathless, in a state of shock.

But quite alive.

"The pistol ball was hollow," Max informed him. "Wax. Rubbed with graphite."

He raised his left hand, thumb elevated. "Filled with blood from this very thumb," he said.

His smile was mirthless, cold. "The other pistol ball was

real," he said, "to throw you off. Misdirection, don't you know. My business."

And he winked at me.

I did not return it. I would not have done so even if I could. *Sonny*, I was thinking with exasperation. *My heart is not constructed of steel, you know.*

"I hope I didn't frighten you again," he said as though reading my thought.

Harry had not spoken a word. Now he was staring at Max uncomprehendingly. I think that, had *his* heart been at risk as well, what Max had just done to him might have finished him off.

In the meantime, Cassandra continued to pound on the door and scream Max's name.

Finally, she added, *"Open the door!"*

Max moved to the desk and tossed the empty pistol on its top. Then, reaching underneath, he pushed the hidden button.

The locking mechanism clicked, the knob was quickly turned, the door flung open, and Cassandra rushed in.

"What the hell is—" she began.

She stopped, aghast, catching sight of Harry on the floor, his shirtfront drenched with blood.

"Oh, my God," she murmured shakily, and ran to him.

Kneeling beside him, she looked at his chest, shuddering at the sight. "My *God*," she said.

"All right," Harry muttered, scarcely able to speak. "I'm all right."

"All *right?*" She stared at him incredulously. "How—"

"Scotch," said Harry, interrupting.

"What *happened?*" she asked.

"Scotch, some Scotch!" he ordered in a rasping voice.

"Yes." She struggled to her feet and hurried toward the bar, glancing apprehensively at Max, who was sitting on the edge of the desk now, quietly observing—as I was, though my quiet was the consequence of a stroke. God only knew what lay behind my son's calmness.

Harry was looking down at his shirt again.

"Jesus Christ," he muttered. With a palsied hand, he tugged a handkerchief from his jacket pocket and dabbed weakly at his shirt.

"What *is* this?" Cassandra demanded of Max.

It was as though she hadn't spoken. Max kicked one foot casually as he sat there. *What is in his* mind? I thought.

Cassandra finished pouring Scotch into a glass and turned from the bar. Returning to Harry, she knelt beside him. Harry took the glass and swallowed half its contents in a single gulp.

He started to cough, eyes watering, and drew in wheezing breaths. Then he downed the rest of the Scotch, shuddering convulsively.

"Can you get up?" Cassandra asked.

He nodded, a feeble stirring of his head. Setting down the glass, he tried to push up, thudding down as his arms gave way.

Grimacing, he rolled to the right and struggled to his knees. "God damn," he muttered.

Cassandra helped him to his feet. He stood unevenly, expression almost blank.

"*What?*" he muttered.

Abruptly, his legs lost strength and he fell to one knee, pulling loose from Cassandra's grip. He twitched, looking startled as he wavered to his left.

"What *is* it?" asked Cassandra.

"I don't . . ." His voice faded as he lost all balance and toppled to one side, crying out in pain as his left elbow banged on the hardwood floor, bearing the brunt of his weight.

He collapsed onto his back, clutching at his elbow, looking dazed.

"What's *happening?*" Cassandra cried.

She knelt beside him hurriedly and tried to help him up.

She couldn't; he had virtually no muscle control remaining. And, newly shocked, I knew exactly what had happened.

Cassandra sensed it too, because she looked accusingly at Max.

"What's happening?" she demanded in a low, trembling voice.

"Nothing much," Max answered cheerfully. "He's dying, that's all."

Oh, Max, I thought. *Son.*

Harry was now too groggy to speak. He tried to sit up. It was impossible. His body was a dead weight, uncoordinated.

"*What have you done to him?*" Cassandra shrieked.

Max smiled.

"Ah, there's the lovely irony, you see," he told her. "I haven't done a thing."

The smile vanished in an instant, leaving his face a mask of implacable venom.

"*You* did," he said.

The smile again, now—terribly—accompanied by a chuckle.

"*And he asked you to*," he finished.

Her gaze jumped to the empty glass.

"Right on," said Max.

Cassandra strained to pull Harry to his feet. "I'll get you to a doctor," she muttered.

"You'd only be driving a corpse into town," Max told her.

She looked at him, appalled. "You bastard," she said. "You absolute bastard."

She saw the impossibility of getting Harry up and, with a

sudden movement, she pushed to her feet and strode quickly toward the entry hall.

Max leaned back and reached beneath the desk. *My God, it isn't over yet!* I thought in dismay. (How little I knew.)

The door swung shut, slammed hard into its frame, and locked itself.

Cassandra stopped in front of it. She tried to open it, then turned, a look of fury on her face.

"And now—" said Max.

Sliding off the desk, he circled it and moved to the mantelpiece, taking down the African blowgun.

"—the *coup de main*," he finished the sentence. "Surprise attack."

He lifted the blowgun to his lips and pointed it at Cassandra.

She shrank back against the door, a look of panic on her face.

Max blew.

Cassandra jolted and gasped. (Inside, I did the same.) She looked down at her chest.

A small feathered dart was protruding from her right breast.

With a sickened noise, she jerked it out and looked at it in disbelief.

A sudden numbness struck her and she dropped it, wavered, slumping back against the door.

Both of them, Max? I thought in horror across the room. Harry was emitting tiny, breathless sounds.

Max set the blowgun back in place above the mantelpiece, then looked at Cassandra.

"I wanted both of you together when I did this," he told her. "Terrorize Harry first, of course. I needed that for my soul's sake.

"But the two of you together for this moment. This most rewarding and fulfilling . . ."

His voice trailed off; he didn't look rewarded *or* fulfilled. He looked completely desolated.

". . . and *tragic* moment," he finished in a broken voice.

Cassandra tried to remain erect, but couldn't.

As though her limbs had been reduced to jelly, she slid downward on the door and landed in a crumpled heap, eyes staring, mouth ajar; a hideous sight. Despite my feelings toward her, I would never have wished this for her.

Harry made a gagging noise, and Max and I looked over at him.

Max walked around the desk and moved to where his agent lay, slowly writhing, eyes—like Cassandra's—staring glassily, breath a failing sibilance.

"So, dear friend," said Max.

Harry tried to lift his head—could not. He stared up sightlessly.

Then his head fell back, thumping on the floor, his eyes closing.

Max knelt to check for a heartbeat.

Satisfied, he stood and moved to where Cassandra half sat, half lay against the door, eyes now closed.

He knelt and pressed a finger underneath her left breast.

"Done," he said, "and *done.*"

Standing quickly, his expression grim, he moved behind the desk and reached beneath it.

The door lock clicked in opening.

Max returned to the door, bent over and, taking hold of Cassandra's arms, pulled her to one side, leaning her body partially against the wall.

He then walked over to me.

"Well, *Padre*," he said. "Had enough for now?"

Could he see in my eyes the pain I felt?

He must have, for he said, "I know; it's terrible." He squeezed my shoulder. "But necessary," he added.

He began to push my wheelchair toward the door.

"Let's get you cleaned up and changed," he said. "Maybe a little lunch."

His tone was so matter-of-fact that I felt more dread than ever.

Just before he opened the door, a distant flash of lightning bleached the shadowy room.

"A storm is on its way," he said.

How was I to know that the nightmare was barely half concluded?

now you see it . . . .

chapter 12

Max took me upstairs on the elevator, wheeled me to my room, and gently cared for me—which meant removing my clothes, cleansing my withered body and re-dressing same.

Throughout all this, he never said a word. I kept looking at his face, hoping that he'd seen the question burning in my eyes.

Why?

If he saw the question—and he must have, being the observant son he always was—he did not elect to answer it. Leaving me to wonder, pained.

Two murders?

Him?

Presently, he took me downstairs once again and rolled my wheelchair to the kitchen. There, he fed me like the child I had become in my eating habits—bib around my neck, spoon scooping up what food I dribbled from my mouth.

All this he did without a word, his expression unreadable—even to me, who had always read him so well.

When I was finished eating, he finally spoke.

"I'm going to leave you in the kitchen for a little while," he said. "I'll be back."

He kissed me on the cheek and left.

I think I felt a tugging at the corners of my eyes; a hint of tears?

Why had he done all this?

Had his need for revenge on Harry and Cassandra been so rabid that he'd been driven to kill them both?

It seemed hard to believe. Max had never been a violent man. Certainly, to me, he had been nothing but a loving son.

Then *why?*

So there I sat in the stillness of the kitchen, bathed, changed, and fed—like the physical infant I'd become. Only my brain remained alert.

Wondering and suffering.

━━━━━▭

How long was it before he came for me? I would estimate the time as half an hour or so, perhaps a little longer.

When he returned to the kitchen, he rolled me back to The Magic Room without a word and set my chair in its customary spot, patted my shoulder, and said, "I hope you'll understand in time, *Padre.*"

With that, he left me there alone . . . as I had been before the nightmare had commenced.

I looked at the desk clock.

It was 2:33 P.M.

A random flicker of lightning continued in the distance, an occasional rumble of thunder. They seemed closer now.

The storm was still approaching.

I looked around the room.

Everything was back in order except for a single detail.

The bloodstains had been wiped up.

The fragments of terra-cotta had been gathered and removed.

The pill vial was gone, presumably returned to the center desk drawer.

The African blowgun was, as noted, restored above mantelpiece.

The pair of dueling pistols had been similarly returned to their places.

The Arabian dagger lay on the desk in its original position.

Four changes had been made.

On the bar, the silver bucket was filled with ice, a bottle of Dom Perignon protruding from its top.

The globe had been covered with a red silk scarf.

The casket was closed.

The Egyptian burial case was closed.

Only one detail deprived the room of orderly appearance.

Still in the same position, crumpled and immobile, lay the body of Cassandra Delacorte.

This I did not understand at all.

Not that I truly understood the reasons for Max's brutal actions.

But this was downright confusing.

Why commit a double murder, hide one body, clean up all the evidence, then leave the other body untouched?

It made no sense.

But then, very little of what happened that day—what had already taken place and what was about to take place—made sense.

At which point—with me utterly perplexed—the lunacy resumed.

In the entry hall, the doorbell rang.

There was no response.

Where is Max? I wondered.

The doorbell rang again.

No response.

Then, as though the person at the door felt that the doorbell wasn't loud enough, he (or she) began to knock.

No answer.

The knocking grew louder.

Soon became a pounding.

Causing a response.

My nerve ends (what was left of them, at any rate) jumped as Cassandra made a feeble sound.

My eyeballs rolled with startled speed.

Her right hand was stirring on the floor.

Now wait a second, said my mind.

The pounding on the front door stopped.

Cassandra moaned a little. Turned her head.

My eyeballs rolled again. (They were to get a real workout that afternoon, let me tell you.)

Outside the house, a man had appeared.

He was in his middle fifties, stocky, dressed in the hat and uniform of the local constabulary, a holstered pistol belted at his portly waist.

He peered into the room, shading his eyes with his left hand.

At first, he only looked around TMR, a frown of curiosity on his thick features.

Then he started, mouth gaping in surprise, as he caught sight of Cassandra.

Immediately, he charged back toward the front door.

Cassandra opened her eyes.

Confusion reigned in me. She wasn't dead—or even incapacitated that I could see.

She had pushed up on one elbow.

As she did, the front door of the house was flung open, crashing against the entry-hall wall.

Cassandra gasped in startlement and looked around.

There was a rapid fall of boots across the entry-hall floor.

Cassandra twitched in alarm as the door was thrown open and the heavy man came bursting in.

He ran to Cassandra and knelt beside her hurriedly.

She stared at him in bewilderment as he helped her to a sitting position.

"Who are you?" she asked. I noticed that her voice was thick, the words slurred; an aftereffect of whatever drug had been on the dart, I assumed.

"Easy," was all the man replied.

He assisted Cassandra to her feet, where she evidenced some difficulty with her balance and the focus of her eyes. "Easy, easy," said the man.

"Who *are* you?" she persisted.

"Sheriff Plum," he answered.

"Plum?" She stared at him for several moments, then pulled away; she immediately began to stagger.

Plum made a sudden move to prevent her fall. *"Easy,"* he said.

She blinked her eyes, grimacing, clearly struggling to regain the use of her senses. She swallowed, and it made a dry sound in her throat.

Disengaging herself once more, she stumbled toward the bar and fell against it, clutching at the top for support.

She stared at the bottles of chilling champagne as though the sight of them was baffling to her.

Then, shaking her head, she moved around the bar, holding on to its top to keep from falling.

Reaching the sink, she turned the faucet arm; cold water splashed down into the stainless-steel basin. Holding on to the sink's edge with her left hand, she cupped her right beneath the fall of water, caught some, and began to wash her face.

At this point, Sheriff Plum, glancing around the room, caught sight of me. "*Oh*, my God," he reacted.

Cassandra, face dripping, looked over at him hurriedly.

"Good afternoon," the Sheriff greeted me.

"He can't answer," Cassandra told him. "He's like a vegetable." (What did I tell you?)

"A *vegetable?*" asked Sheriff Plum in a surprised voice.

"He had a stroke many years ago," she explained, her voice still slurring words. "He can't talk or move; ignore him."

Which was pretty much my status in her mind.

"But—" Sheriff Plum gave up on me and looked back at Cassandra, who was drying her face with a bar towel.

"What's going on here?" he asked.

She looked at him, then turned her head and scanned the room.

Each sight she saw appeared to puzzle her further. She rubbed her forehead hard as though to activate the gray cells underneath her skull. Ran her hands across her breasts as though to verify their presence.

"Are you all right?" the Sheriff asked.

Cassandra looked at him, disoriented. "Where did you come from?" she asked.

"What?" The question seemed bewildering to him.

She repeated it more demandingly.

"From *town*," he said, still looking puzzled.

"I mean—" she broke off with an angry grimace "—who let you in?" she finished.

He looked more confused than ever.

"*No one* let me in," he said. "The front door was unlocked. I came in by myself because I saw you lying on the floor in here and thought you were the 'one'—"

He stopped as though perplexity was overwhelming him.

"Who got murdered, then?" he asked.

chapter 13

Cassandra did not reply at first. She stared at him, her features very nearly blank.

Finally, she asked, "How did *you* know about it?"

"Someone telephoned my office," he replied.

"Telephoned your office?" (She was totally confounded now. So was I.)

"Yes—"

She interrupted him abruptly.

"My husband's agent," she declared.

"Your husband's agent telephoned my office?" asked the Sheriff.

"No!" she cried in agitation. "My husband's agent is the one who got murdered!"

"He's the one . . ." Plum's voice faded as he watched her curiously.

She'd begun to pace around, shaking her head and blinking hard.

"You want me to call for an ambulance?" he asked.

Cassandra stopped, wavering, and turned to face him.

"My husband did it," she told him.

"Your husband—"

"—*did* it," she cut him off.

He stared at her as though devoid of comprehension.

"Did you *hear* me?" she demanded.

"*Yes*," he answered. "You said . . ."

His voice trailed off again as though he hadn't inkling-one regarding what she'd said.

Cassandra ground her teeth together. She did that when she was furious.

"*My-husband-murdered-his-agent*," she said slowly, spacing each word evenly, enunciating clearly.

Plum's eyes narrowed. "You *witnessed* it?" he asked.

"Yes! Of course I did! Why else—"

Suddenly, she stopped and looked around the room.

"No, wait," she said. "He wouldn't do that. It wouldn't make sense."

The Sheriff was as nonplussed as I was, except that he could verbalize it.

"What wouldn't make sense?" he asked.

Cassandra threw off momentary confusion with a willful scowl.

"I want you to arrest my husband," she told the Sheriff. "I'll testify to what I saw."

The Sheriff's expression did not, in any way, reflect a bulb turning on.

"Which was what?" he asked. (*Rustic idiot,* I thought.)

"I just *told* you!" snapped Cassandra, teeth grinding again. "My husband murdered his agent. *Poisoned* him!"

"*Poisoned?*" said the newly startled Plum; clearly, he could only deal with one brief bit of information at a time.

"*Yes*," said Cassandra. "*Yes. Yes.* Arrest him and I'll testify against him."

"Regarding what?" he asked as though trying very hard to get it straight in his brain. *Who elected this dolt?* I wondered.

"You *still* don't understand?" Cassandra said, incredulous.

Her insulting tone made him bristle.

"I mean, regarding *how* it happened," he responded sharply. *"Where* it happened. *When* it happened. And if you have any notions about it, *why* it happened."

The demands, though scarcely a barrage of them, seemed too much for Cassandra now. Shaking her head fitfully, she returned to the bar, lifted a handful of cracked ice to her face and rubbed it over her forehead as though to chill alertness and perception into returning.

Plum and I observed. I didn't know what the worthy Sheriff was thinking, but as for me, I was trying hard to fathom why Max would commit murder (down to one now), then notify the law and have it show up at his house.

I had to assume that it was done in a desire to pay for his crime.

Boy, was *I* wrong.

�◼▭

Done, Cassandra dumped the ice back into the bucket, blew warm breath on her palm, then turned to the Sheriff.

"I'm sorry," she said. "Apparently I'm still drugged."

"Drugged?" the Sheriff echoed, perplexity renewed.

She couldn't hold her tongue. (I wonder if I could have.) "Did you think I was taking a *nap* on the floor?" she asked.

"Now see here—" Sheriff Plum looked grievously offended.

"All right, I'm sorry," Cassandra said. "Forget it. I want you to arrest my husband for the murder of his agent."

"Where did this happen?" the Sheriff asked.

"In this room," Cassandra answered.

He gazed at her—much like a cow, it occurred to me—obviously waiting for elaboration.

She pointed across the room.

"My husband's agent was sitting on the floor there. I thought he'd been shot—"

She broke off, wincing. "No, forget that," she said, "it's not important."

"*Not important?*" Plum looked shocked.

"I'll explain it later," she responded tightly. "The point is that my husband's agent was sitting on the floor over there when I brought him a glass of Scotch."

"Wait a second," Plum objected. "*You* brought him a glass of Scotch? I thought you said—"

"I didn't know it was poisoned!" Cassandra cried. "Obviously, my *husband* had poisoned the Scotch! His agent was upset by what had happened—*I'll explain it later!*" She cut Plum off. "Anyway, his agent asked me for a glass of Scotch, so I gave it to him. *I had no idea it was poisoned.*"

Sheriff Plum was rubbing his chin, his expression making it clear that all this was unclear to him.

"Do you *get* it?" Cassandra pleaded, looking at him with an expression halfway between appeal and contempt.

"Listen—" he started.

She couldn't, and rushed on. "*Where* did it happen? In this room. *When* did it happen?" She looked at her wristwatch, blinking exaggeratedly to make the tiny numbers come into focus. "Approximately two hours ago. *Why* did it—"

"*Two hours?*" Plum was aghast. "Why wasn't I told sooner?"

"I was *unconscious!*"

"What about the man who called me?"

"I have no idea who called you! It must have been my husband, but why should *he* call you?"

My question exactly, I thought.

Cassandra's voice had gotten very shrill, and the Sheriff gestured to calm her down.

"Take it easy," he cautioned.

"How can I take it easy when my husband is a murderer?" she cried.

"Okay, okay," said Plum. "Let's get some evidence going, then."

He gestured toward the room. "Where were you located when it happened?"

"Lying on the floor over there," she answered, pointing toward the entry-hall door.

He winced as though reluctant to ask for elucidation lest it bring back confusion. But he had to know.

"And why were you . . . lying over there?" he asked.

Cassandra's sigh was heavy. She must have seen no end to this; *I* didn't. Still, it had to be dealt with eventually.

"Because I'd been shot," she told him.

Seeing the flare of eye-glazed bewilderment on his face, she added quickly, "Not with a gun! With a *blow*gun!"

He stared at her.

"Oh, God," she murmured.

Still, trying, she pointed toward the fireplace.

"You see the African blowgun hanging over the mantelpiece?" she asked.

Sheriff Plum looked in that direction. His expression did not indicate dawning perception.

"That thing hanging on the wall above the fireplace?" she asked. "Over the two dueling pistols?"

"Dueling pistols," he muttered, still no glimmer in his eyes.

"That *long* thing?" she said, voice rising, "like a *tube*? A *wooden tube*?"

"Oh, yes," he said.

"Thank God," she murmured.

"Now, see here, ma'am," he began.

"That's what I was shot with," she informed him, covering his words with hers. "It had a poisoned dart in it. No, no, I take that back! I don't mean poison!" she added desperately, noticing a new confusion on his face. "Obviously, it wasn't poison or I'd be dead. It must have had some kind of drug on its point. Something that paralyzed me, knocked me out. That's why—"

She stopped, staring unbelievingly at the blankness of his expression. *Local politics are at a very low ebb*, I thought.

"This is going to last forever," she mumbled.

You know, by now, how little regard I held for this woman. It is the measure of Plum's density that I actually felt sorry for Cassandra.

She was watching as the Sheriff walked to the fireplace and took down the blowgun. He held it up to the window light to peer through it. "No dart," he said.

"Do you actually think he'd put it *back* in there?" she snapped.

"Mrs. Delacorte, you're giving me a lot of things to digest all at once," the Sheriff said; he was beginning to sound a little grumpy now. "Let's try to be polite to one another, shall we?"

Maybe there is a brain inside there somewhere, I thought. *Deep inside, of course.*

"You're right, I'm sorry," Cassandra repented. "It's just that I'm so upset."

"Of course you are." He nodded. "Very well then. You were hit with a blowgun dart that had some kind of drug in its point—is that what you're telling me?"

"That's what I told you," she responded, watching him return the blowgun to its spot above the mantelpiece.

"Now we're getting somewhere," he said.

I saw Cassandra cast an imploring look to the heavens just before Plum turned back to her.

"Where did it hit you?" he asked.

"Does it really matter?" she retorted.

"I'd like to know, yes," he told her.

"Here," she said, prodding an index finger at her right breast. (Was that a wince of embarrassment I saw on Plum's face?)

He swallowed. "You're lucky it didn't hit you in the eye."

Cassandra chose not to respond to that. What could she have said? "That's a really stupid remark, Sheriff"?

"And your husband shot this—*blew* this dart at you?"

"*Yes. Yes.* To keep me from leaving the room after he'd poisoned Harry—"

She broke off as the Sheriff raised his hand as though to stop the traffic flow of new information.

"Harry?" he asked.

"*My husband's agent*," Cassandra answered.

"You never told me his name before," he said.

"Oh, yes. All right. I'm *sorry*."

"Okay," he said. "Let's get this straightened out, then."

I know he heard her pitiful groan but decided to ignore it.

"Harry was sitting on the floor over there. You gave him the poisoned Scotch. Did he die right away?"

"No. I tried to get him on his feet to take him to the hospital. I couldn't though; he had no control of his limbs."

"All right." Plum nodded gravely. "Now we're getting somewhere."

Was that a pitiful groan I heard in my own throat? Probably imagination. But the man was driving me nuts, along with Cassandra.

"You tried to leave the room—"

"To call your office," she interrupted.

"It was *you* who called my office?"

"*No!*" she cried. "I said I was *going* to call your office! But before I could, my husband hit me with the dart!"

"Got you," he said. "And that paralyzed you."

"Yes. And I fell down."

"And saw this Harry—"

"Kendal. Harry Kendal."

"Harry Kendal, right." He nodded. "Now I'm getting the picture."

Harry's words flared brightly in my brain. *Jesus H. Christ!*

"You saw this Harry Kendal die before you lost consciousness?"

"Yes!"

"*Okay.*" He tried to mollify her with a gesture. "I've got it now."

He frowned. "Except—"

A look of pained vexation took her face.

"—you said before, you thought this Harry Kendal had been shot."

"Oh." She nodded. "Yes. Apparently what happened was that my husband terrorized Harry with—"

"Terrorized?" he broke in.

"I said *apparently* because he fired one of those dueling pistols at him."

"Then—"

"*Let me finish,*" she demanded, begging. "The pistol ball was obviously a fake one—made of wax, hollow, filled with blood. A magician's gimmick."

"I see," said Plum. "And why would he do that?"

"I told you—to terrorize Harry."

Plum's voice seemed suddenly—surprisingly—aware as he inquired, "And why would he want to do that, Mrs. Delacorte?"

chapter 14

Cassandra didn't—couldn't—speak at first. Then she answered, "I don't know." Of course she did; we both did now. But she had no intention of letting the Sheriff know.

"No idea?" he asked; much as though he suspected the truth, although he obviously couldn't have.

Cassandra tried deflection.

"Look, does any of this really matter?" she demanded. "My-husband-murdered-his-agent. *Arrest* him."

"Please," said Plum, "let me decide what matters and what doesn't matter."

She could only sigh in response. Heavily.

"All right." He looked around. "Where *is* your husband then? I'd like to talk with him."

"*Talk* with him?" She looked insulted. "What is there to *talk* about? *He murdered Harry Kendal.* Period!"

"Mrs. Delacorte," he said, "these things have to be done in a certain way. I can't just arrest a man because—"

"—some stupid woman tells you that he murdered someone," she broke in coldly.

"That's *not* what I was about to say," he told her.

He blew out a cheek-puffing breath.

"Assuming that what you say is true—" he began.

"*Assuming?*" she raged.

"*—do you have any idea where this agent's body might be?*" he finished strongly.

She was taken aback by the question. So was I. I hadn't even thought about it.

"No," Cassandra told him as though the thought had just occurred to her as well. "I don't. I just—"

She stopped with a scowl. "How could I *possibly* know?" she asked, affronted. "I've been *unconscious.*"

"All right," he said. "Is there any place we might begin to search for it? For *him*," he amended.

Cassandra was about to answer when she held back, narrowing her eyes.

She looked around the room, a curious expression on her face. I wondered what she was doing.

Plum also wondered. "Why are you looking around the room?" he asked.

She didn't reply, her gaze moving slowly around TMR.

"Mrs. Delacorte?"

"I can't believe—" she started.

She twitched at a rumble of thunder.

Now Plum was looking around the room. So was I—as best my eyeballs could manage; I wasn't a damn iguana though, with a hundred-and-eighty-degree vision in each eye.

"What are you thinking?" the Sheriff asked. "That the body's in *here?*"

He looked at one of the walls.

"Are there secret panels or something?" he asked.

"It wouldn't make sense," Cassandra murmured to herself.

Her eyes focused on Plum. "What?" she inquired. "Secret panels?"

"Yes. I thought maybe—"

The Sheriff's voice broke off as Cassandra moved abruptly to the wall panel she'd used earlier to get rid of Brian when he was made up as her.

Pressing at a section of molding, she caused the panel to open. (In a way, I hated that this stranger should be privy to a secret I'd created in this house almost forty years before.)

Cassandra had moved through the opening to look inside. Plum moved to the opening as well and peered in.

He jerked back as Cassandra came out, looking angry (at herself).

"Of course he wouldn't put Harry in there," she said. "That would be ridiculous."

"Is this the only secret panel?" asked Plum.

"As far as I know," she said, closing the panel.

That surprised me. Had Max made other alterations to this room that I didn't know about? The notion was disturbing to me.

"What do you mean, as far as you know?" Plum was obviously thinking along the same lines. "Isn't this your house?"

"My house, yes. My private study, no. My husband calls it his Magic Room. As far as I know, he could have had it gimmicked in a dozen different ways without my knowing it."

Disturbing, I thought.

"I guess it's time I talked to *him,* then," Plum said. "Do you know where he might be?"

She looked newly aggravated. *"Sheriff,"* she said. "How many times do I have to tell you? I was *unconscious!"*

"How do you expect me to *arrest* him, then?" he charged. "If we don't even know where he is!"

She thought about it for several moments, then replied,

"Wouldn't it be better if we found Harry's body first? Until we do, my husband is just going to deny everything."

"You think he'll deny it," said Plum.

"Well, you don't imagine he'll *confess*, do you?" she demanded.

Yes, I do imagine that, I answered silently. *He's not a man to shirk responsibility.*

Sheriff Plum was losing patience now.

"Mrs. Delacorte," he said, "I don't *know* your husband. He might do *anything*, as far as I'm concerned."

Touché, you clod, I thought.

Cassandra looked apologetic. "You're right. I'm sorry," she said.

Her features hardened then.

"Well, believe me, he *will* deny it," she said. "He didn't set this whole cabal up only to admit his guilt."

"Cabal?" asked Plum.

"*Plot,*" she told him. "Secret plan. Conspiracy. Maneuver—"

"*Got* it!" cried the Sheriff. "*Lordamighty!*"

Lordamighty?

"I'll take your word that he won't confess," Plum went on. "So what do—"

She cut him off. "We have to find Harry's body," she said. "If we can only—"

She stopped, looking across the room.

At the burial case.

The Sheriff asked, "What's that?"

"An Egyptian burial case," she told him.

"From Egypt?"

"Well, maybe it's from Yugoslavia, I don't know," she snapped.

"There's no need to be smart," the Sheriff told her.

Especially for you, I thought. (*Max, where* are *you?* is what I was thinking behind that thought.)

Cassandra had exhaled wearily. *"Sorry,"* she said. She didn't sound it.

"I think, before we start searching for a body—I'll probably need a warrant anyway—I'd better speak to your husband," the Sheriff decided.

"It's always kept open," she said.

He squinted at her. *"What?"* he asked.

Cassandra walked across the room and opened the burial case.

"Yes, it would have been terribly clever of him to hide the body in here," she said, scowling at the empty interior.

Neither of them noticed what was happening behind them.

On the right glove of the suit of armor.

A large drop of blood was about to drip from one of its fingertips.

"Where might I be likely to find your husband, Mrs. Delacorte?" the Sheriff asked.

Her smile was bitter. "After committing murder?" she said. "On a flight to Europe, probably."

No, I thought; *not Max.* But it was only half a thought.

The bulk of my attention was on the suit of armor as the hanging drop of blood disengaged itself from the fingertip of the glove and dropped to the floor, splashing delicately. They did not react.

Can't you hear *that?* I thought incredulously.

"You think he's left, then?" the Sheriff asked. Obviously, he hadn't heard.

"Sheriff, how am I supposed to know?" Cassandra replied. "How *could* I know?"

Obviously, she hadn't heard either.

Now a second drop of blood was collecting at the tip of the glove finger. I watched with a kind of sickened fascination as it stretched downward, quivered, broke away, then fell to the floor, where it splashed on the damp spot left by the first falling drop of blood.

Are the two of you deaf? screamed my mind.

Apparently so. Plum was walking over to the casket now. "This a trick?" he asked, pointing at it.

"No, it's real," Cassandra said. "At least he says it is."

"*Real?*" He looked repelled. "A real coffin in your husband's office?"

Magic Room! I cried out. Minus sound, of course.

"That's the kind of man he is," Cassandra answered him.

Folks! I thought.

Plum peered in through the glass top, twitching in shock as he saw what he thought was Max.

"Is this *him?*" he asked, aghast.

"Of *course* not," she said, frowning. "It's a quarter-size dummy."

Plum grimaced, looking ill. "Sure *looks* real," he said.

He turned to ask her something else and saw her staring at the suit of armor. *God bless us all,* I was thinking—

—as a third, large drop of blood was disconnecting from the fingertip of the glove.

They both winced simultaneously as it splattered on the floor. Now *you hear it,* I thought, *at last.*

"My God," said Plum.

Cassandra's expression was one of disbelieving horror.

"He *wouldn't,*" she said.

Plum started toward the suit of armor.

"It wouldn't make sense," Cassandra murmured shakily. I had to agree.

But who was in the suit of armor, then?

"Why do you keep saying that?" asked Plum.

"Because he's a *magician,*" she explained. "He'd never be so obvious."

That, at least, she understands, I thought.

But she wasn't certain enough to not watch apprehensively as Plum reached the suit of armor and stopped.

A fourth drop of blood was collecting at the fingertip.

Plum winced again—as Cassandra did—when the drop fell, enlarging the scarlet splash-mark on the floor.

Gingerly, he reached up toward the faceplate, his movement slow, almost diffident. Cassandra watched him with a sickened gaze.

Plum's fingers moved closer to the faceplate.

Closer.

chapter 15

Astonishment!

Plum recoiled, crying out involuntarily as the suit of armor sprang open, its hinged halves stopping with a loud, metallic clang.

Cassandra jerked back, gasping.

And I recoiled and jerked back inwardly, my mind crying out—

—as *The Great Delacorte* stepped forth.

He was attired in full illusionist regalia—white tie and tails, a top hat accordioned shut in his hands. His smile was broad, theatrical.

He was, in fact, not standing before us so much as making an appearance, his expression that which a generation of magic devotees had come to know so well—genial, urbane, and welcoming.

"Good afternoon, my friends!" he said. *The Great Delacorte* saluted them.

Despite my startlement and general disconcertment, it warmed my heart to see him like that.

This was a far different Maximilian Delacorte from the man who met with Harry Kendal—had it only been a few short hours ago?

That Delacorte was wan and understated, soft-spoken until righteous anger came. That was a hurt, embittered Delacorte, a man nearly broken by inner pain.

The man who stood before us now was, indeed, *The Great Delacorte.*

And more.

This man was *on.* Keyed up. Imbued with energy. One might put it, in the current lexicon, that he was *wired.*

There was an undercurrent of almost crazed ebullience in his look and manner which transcended even his usually effusive stage persona.

But then, something *more* was going on beneath the surface.

Frozen by surprise, both Cassandra and the Sheriff twitched as Max popped open his top hat, set it on his head, and tapped it into place.

"It will be my pleasure this afternoon," he said high-spiritedly, "to entertain you with some minor whimsies of illusion . . . some larger feats of prestidigitation . . . and some exploits of darker magic which will place each one of you— whether you will or not—*In Touch* with the Mysterious."

Crystals of icy dread began to assail my inner warmth.

This had been the opening speech of his act (virtually the opening speech of *my* act, too) for fourteen years.

At the conclusion of which (as he did now), he tossed up a cloud of golden dust which crackled brilliantly, then vanished into thin air.

Plum had twitched at this. He stared at Max, mouth open.

Max swept off his top hat, bowing regally.

"I do not believe we've met, sir," he observed.

Plum was speechless. So was I. (Well, I always was.) I could not escape a chilling premonition that Max had truly gone insane. Under all the circumstances, wasn't it a possibility?

Max tilted his head inquisitively toward the Sheriff. "Sir?" he said.

Plum swallowed quickly, clearing his throat. "Grover Plum," he said. "Sheriff, Medfield County."

"Well, Sheriff, Medfield County," Max replied. "So good to meet you."

His expression became that of a man savoring some new, delightful knowledge.

"*Grover Plum*," he said. "How musical a name."

He beamed. "I am, of course, Maximilian Delacorte, known professionally as The *Great . . .* Delacorte."

He confused me further by gesturing expansively in my direction, adding, "And this, of course, is my beloved father, the *original Great Delacorte*, a magician of worldwide distinction and renown."

"I . . . met him," mumbled Plum.

"Glad to hear it, Sheriff," Max responded.

Offhandedly, he gestured toward Cassandra, who was looking toward him with a dark, despising disdain. (How's that for alliteration?)

"You've already met Miss Crane," he said.

"*Who?*" the Sheriff asked.

Max pointed at Cassandra as though at the target for a firing squad. "That *woman*," he said. "Her maiden name was Crane."

His cheeks puffed outward noticeably as he made a sound of sardonic amusement.

"*Maiden*," he said, "a title nonapplicable to her for many decades."

Cassandra tightened and began to speak. He cut her off.

"What brings you here so soon?" Max asked the Sheriff.

"It was *you* who telephoned my office, then," said Plum.

"Of course," said Max. "I didn't expect you so promptly though."

"I'm not surprised," the Sheriff said, "since you didn't mention murder in your call."

Max's smile was evanescent. "No, I didn't," he admitted.

"Why did you kill him, Max?" Cassandra asked.

He did not reply. Reshutting the suit of armor with care, he strode to the bar, placed his top hat on its surface and gave the chilling bottle of Dom Perignon a few quick turns between his palms.

"Champagne, Sheriff?" he offered.

"I hardly think this is the time for champagne," responded Plum.

"Oh. Too bad," said Max.

He glanced at Cassandra. "My dear?" he asked. His tone became cajoling. "Your favorite brand."

"I don't drink to murder," she told him in a throaty, malignant voice.

He smiled. "Too bad," he said again. "Not the comment though. That was very good." He pointed at her with approval. *"Telling."*

"Mister Delacorte—" Plum started.

"We'll have the champagne later, then," Max said. "When we're ready."

"Mister Delacorte—" Plum began again.

"Perhaps with caviar," Max said. "Oh, I'm sorry, Sheriff. Did I interrupt you?"

"I'd like to remind you—" said the Sheriff.

"Uno momento," Max broke in.

Moving briskly to the Egyptian burial case, he shut the lid, then turned back with a smile.

"Like to keep a tidy household," he said cheerfully.

Max, what is going on in your mind?! I thought in deep distress.

The Sheriff had begun to bristle now.

"See here, Mister Delacorte," he said, "I'm not here on a social visit. My office gets a call, I drive out here and find your wife lying on the floor over there."

"You *do?*" said Max. He turned to Cassandra with a look of innocent curiosity. "Why were you lying on the floor, darling?" he asked.

"Where is he, Max?" she cried.

His tone was bland as he inquired, "Who's that, my dear?"

Her cheeks were whitening with rage. (Clearly, he was still exacting vengeance on her.) "Stop the stupid game, Max!" she demanded. "We're not playing! Where *is* he?"

"I think you'd better tell us, Mister Delacorte," the Sheriff added.

Max looked at him.

"Your wife claims you're the one who committed the murder," said Plum.

Max's expression became one of "hurt" bewilderment.

"What a dreadful thing to say," he responded.

He looked at Cassandra, clucking with reproach.

"How awful," he said.

She looked at him with disbelief now.

"You asked him here to kill him," she said, a look of genuine pain on her face. "To *kill* him."

Max's mouth was opening to reply when Sheriff Plum said, "Let's get down to details now, shall we, Mister Delacorte?"

He removed a pad and stubby pencil from the breast pocket of his shirt. Max looked at it approvingly.

"By all means!" he said; he actually sounded enthusiastic. "I'm a detail man myself; always have been. Nothing to compare with details, is there? Without details—"

"Stop it," Cassandra cut him off, her voice low-pitched, almost murderous.

Max looked at her, then made a casual noise which I interpreted as asking, "What on earth is bothering you, my dear?"

As the Sheriff began to question him, Max removed four playing cards from his left trouser pocket and started to perform a back-and-front palm with them. The sight made me uneasy as I recalled the difficulty he'd had with the billiard-ball replication earlier.

"This Mister—" Plum began.

"Kendal. Harry Kendal," Max provided, one of the playing cards between the thumb and forefinger of his right hand.

He made a slight downward movement, followed by an upward movement which allowed the card to fall across the back of his first, second and third fingers, the little finger rising to the edge of the card. (Despite my uneasiness, the magician in me was absorbed completely by his hands.)

Rapidly, his forefinger replaced the thumb, his fingers were extended, and the card vanished from the palm, all in the space of a second. Seeing this, I felt a sense of relief for him.

"K-e-n-d—" Sheriff Plum was writing down the letters with laborious effort.

"—a-l," completed Max. "Kendal. Very good."

As he turned back his hand, he closed his fingers into the palm and gripped the center of the card with his thumb, opening the four fingers outward until the card was gripped against the two middle fingers and vanished from the back of his hand as well. *Good, Max,* I thought automatically.

"What time did he get here?" the Sheriff asked.

Max was repeating the back-and-front palm, the cards appearing, disappearing, then appearing once again.

"Who's that?" he asked in a distracted voice.

"Don't let him do this to you, Sheriff," warned Cassandra.

chapter 16

Cassandra's remark made Max almost drop the card.

He winced, then directed a forced smile at the Sheriff.

"Does this bother you?" he asked. "It's just a habit."

"I *said*, what time did Harry Kendal get here?" Plum repeated the query.

"Darling?" Max inquired sweetly. "You were here when he arrived. I was out walking, you recall."

As he spoke, he fanned the four cards with his right hand, then let them drop into his palm.

Cassandra regarded him balefully.

"Just past noon," she told the Sheriff.

"Thank you, precious," said Max, bringing up his right hand to his left as though to transfer the cards, then palming them in his right and closing his left as though they contained the cards.

"*You murdering bastard.*" Cassandra glared at him. "If you think you're going to get away with this . . ."

Max made a sound of disapproval at her language, quickly grasping the corners of the cards with his right thumb and bending them over so he could pass the hand, fingers open, across the back of his left hand.

All of this took place in rapid order as the conversation progressed; a skilled magician's feat.

"Why did he come to see you?" asked Plum.

"Well—" Max dropped his left hand casually, displayed the empty left hand, then produced the card with a fan from behind his right knee "—he came to talk about business," he said. "An engagement in Las Vegas. Wasn't that it, babe?" He smiled falsely at Cassandra.

She didn't answer, watching him with hooded eyes.

The Sheriff watched with displeasure as Max repeated the card manipulations.

I watched Max with a coldness in my stomach, wondering what he was up to, what he had in mind, what *plan*. I knew there had to be one.

"Second method," Max was saying as he demonstrated. "Hold the cards between the right forefinger and thumb and pass the left hand across the front of the right as though taking hold of them. Under cover of the left hand, quickly back-palm them behind the right. Your audience—"

"I'd prefer you didn't do that, Mister Delacorte," the Sheriff told him.

"*Really?*" Max sounded surprised. "You don't like it, Grover? You don't think it's jolly? *Legerdemain?* Sleight of hand?"

"*Mr. Delacorte—*"

Max fumbled, almost dropping the cards.

With a scowl, he made them vanish, slipping them into his trouser pocket. He looked at Plum with a goading expression.

"I'm all ears, Grover," he said in a hardened voice. "*Hit me.*"

"Why did you have to kill him, Max?" Cassandra asked.

There was an aching in her voice now which made him look at her strangely.

"Did Mister Kendal leave the house?" the Sheriff asked.

"I've already told you!" Cassandra's anger burst out. "Harry Kendal was *murdered!*"

The Sheriff tried to curb his irritation.

"I would like to hear what your husband has to say, Mrs.—"

"He'll say anything to throw you off!" she interrupted, raging.

Again, she looked at Max, her tone despairing.

"You didn't have to *kill* him, Max," she said.

Max, admit it, I thought. *Be done with this.*

Cassandra turned and walked to the picture window, looking out at the gazebo by the lake, her features taut.

"To repeat the question, Mister Delacorte," said Plum. "Did Harry Kendal—"

"Harry Kendal vacated these premises—under his own power, I might add—I *will* add—I *did* add—at approximately a quarter after one."

"He's lying," Cassandra said without turning.

He *was* lying. But *why?*

The Sheriff was writing in his pad. "One . . . fifteen," he said.

"Another way of putting it, but just as good," Max said.

The Sheriff threw him a frowning glance. "I'm not amused, Mister Delacorte," he said.

"Nor should you be," concurred my son.

Cassandra turned abruptly and walked to the spot where Harry had been lying after drinking the Scotch.

Kneeling, she began to examine the floorboards.

"Looking for something, darling?" Max inquired.

"You'll know when I find it," she answered coldly.

"Looking forward to it, snookums," Max responded.

He watched Plum writing on his pad.

"Did you know," he said, "that when one is blindfolded, one can see past one's nose?"

Plum glanced at him with disinterest. *Now what?* I thought.

"*But*," continued Max as though the information must be absolutely fascinating to the Sheriff, "until one needs that sight, one keeps one's eyes *shut*, don't you see? In that way, one need not feign blindness during that period, because one is genuinely blind. *N'est-ce pas?*"

I felt a sense of melancholic pain, remembering the very day I'd told that to my thirteen-year-old son.

Plum had frowned at the remark. "What has that got to do with what we're talking about?" he asked.

Max smiled benignly. "Nothing," he said. (*Does he have a plan?* I wondered.)

The Sheriff drew in a tight breath.

"I'm getting tired of this, Mister Delacorte," he said.

"Here's an intriguing item, Grover," said Max, raising his right index finger as though testing the wind. "The magician, dressed in blue, rides a horse onto the stage, accompanied by a number of attendants dressed in white."

His next words faded from my hearing as, abruptly, I was on the stage again, on horseback, dressed in blue. A screen was raised for several seconds, then removed. *Voila!* I'd vanished into thin air, the attendants running the horse offstage. Applause; delighted laughter.

The answer was, of course, simplicity itself. While behind the screen, I jumped from the horse, ripped off my paper costume and stuffed it into a pocket. Underneath, I was dressed in white, like the attendants. No one ever noticed.

"*Pourquoi?*" Max's final words grew audible to me. "In

the ensuing rush of movement, no one takes the time to count the number of attendants."

The Sheriff was glaring at him now; that made a pair of glares. (You know where the other one came from.)

"You understand?" asked Max. "Leading your audience into seeing what you want them to see."

Cassandra looked up from her rapt perusal of the floor-boards.

"How long are you going to let him do this, Sheriff?" she asked, standing.

"Listen, Mister Delacorte," Plum started to say.

He broke off, tightening resentfully as Max began a rapid single-card production, speaking as he worked.

"Back-palm ten cards in the right hand. Bend the fingers in. Reach across with Right One, press against the top card."

"Mister Delacorte—"

"Disengage the card from the pack by pressing down and in with thumb pad as you straighten out the fingers."

"Damn it," said the Sheriff.

"*Wait*," Max said. "Let the card slip down between Right One and Right Two, through Five, until all the cards have been produced."

He started to do the same thing with his left hand. "Back-palm ten cards in the left hand," he began.

"*Delacorte.*" The Sheriff's cheeks were getting pink.

"All tricks must be done in threes, you know," my son nonsequitured, the expression on his face not entirely sane now, I saw with dismay.

"Card tricks. Coin tricks. Ball tricks. *All* tricks." The cards kept appearing one by one in the fingers of his left hand. "Tear paper three times. Tap tables and containers three times. Announce illusions three times. This creates a deep response, you see. Beginning, middle, end." His eyes were positively glittering. "Father, Mother, Holy Ghost. Eternal—*damn it!*"

I started inwardly as his voice flared when he lost hold of the cards, which scattered to the floor like falling birds. He kicked them aside in a burst of fury.

Cassandra looked delighted by his failure.

"You have just enjoyed the privilege of seeing *The Great Delacorte* in performance," she said. "Thrilling, wasn't it?"

Max gave her a quick, acerbic look, then turned back to Plum as the Sheriff spoke, his voice antagonistic.

"Would you rather we continued this at my office?" Plum asked.

"No," said Max immediately. "I prefer to be here."

"Let's *do* it then," snapped Plum.

Max gestured loosely. (Was he back again, or farther adrift? I couldn't tell.)

"What can I tell you?" he inquired. "That my wife is loony? It's a fact. There's been no murder here."

"Liar!" Cassandra shouted. "You killed Harry right in front of me!"

Max looked bemused. "I *did?*" he said. "Maybe I should reevaluate. Maybe I've got amnesia."

He was still playing the game, then. Dementedly perhaps, but in control of his faculties.

"For God's sake, take him in!" Cassandra told the Sheriff. "I'll testify against him."

"Wives can't testify against their husbands, darling," Max reminded her. "I must say, you're behaving most erratically."

"I think we'd better take a drive into town," the Sheriff said. "If you want to get a coat or something . . ."

Max looked at him without expression.

Abruptly, a red ball appeared in his right hand, and he tossed it into the air. Plum lowered his eyes involuntarily as it fell to the floor and bounced. So did Cassandra.

"See how his gaze followed the ball, my friends," said Max, addressing an unseen audience. "Unexpected movement, you see."

"Never mind the—" started Plum.

He stopped, eyes shifting suddenly as Max produced a burning match in his left hand. (I remembered teaching him that.)

"Again," said Max, "his gaze caught by the movement, by the flame."

The Sheriff grimaced and was about to speak when Max turned quickly to his right, gasping as he looked upward. Plum glanced at the same spot.

"Again." Max smiled. "His line of sight directed."

His arm shot out as he pointed across the room. *"There!"* he cried.

The Sheriff began to turn, then looked back willfully, his face a mask of anger. "Damn it, Delacorte!"

"You see," said Max, striding toward Cassandra, "I can decide, at any moment, what he will or will not look at."

Cassandra drew back in alarm as Max walked up to her.

Reaching down, he jerked apart the front of her blouse, revealing her large, brassiere-cupped breasts. *Max!* I thought in shock.

Cassandra gasped and snatched at the blouse to cover herself, her face hardened with fury.

A startled Plum was gaping at the sight.

"How's that for misdirection, Grover?" asked my son. "At the moment you got an eyeful of my wife's knockers, I could have walked a purple elephant past you without you seeing it."

He glanced at me. "Forgive me, *Padre*," he said. "I was only making a point."

Cassandra was fastening her blouse now, an odd expression on her face, no longer furious, but grimly thoughtful.

"You didn't have time, did you?" she asked.

Max elevated his eyebrows. "Pardon?"

"You didn't have time to put the body anywhere outside," she said. "It has to be in the house."

Plum stared at her in confusion.

And Harry's voice was heard.

"Well, it took you long enough to guess that, babe," he said.

chapter 17

The Sheriff looked around in startlement.

"Who said that?" he asked.

Cassandra moved abruptly to the globe and snatched off the red silk scarf.

She jolted with shock (as, somewhere in my dead bod, I did too), grimacing exaggeratedly.

Plum stared at the globe in revulsion.

Inside was Harry Kendal's head, now hacked off at the neck, veins and arteries dangling, features gray and bloodless, eyes staring.

"*What the hell is that?*" asked Plum.

He twitched as the head responded.

"Hi there, Sheriff," it said. "Harry Kendal here. Well, not exactly here. Part of me is elsewhere. My body's cabbing back to Boston with a different head on it. Plastic. Stuffed with shredded contracts—Delacorte's, of course; all canceled. Head looks pretty good. First class. Hat fits perfectly. I doubt if anyone will notice."

The head turned. Harry's dead eyes seemed to look directly at Cassandra.

"Hi, babe," he said. "Remember the Essex House? Room Five-twenty-five? Hanh? Hanh? Did I give good head or didn't I?"

The head emitted a hideous, gargling laugh, the gray lips drawn back sharply. *Oh, Max,* I thought.

Then the eyes fell shut, the face of the head went still.

"You filthy, sadistic son of a bitch," Cassandra said.

I almost agreed with her.

Max smiled at Plum and gestured toward the globe.

"Holography," he said. "A wonderful invention. Enabling us to bring new life to old illusions."

He looked at me. "If only you could have had it, *Padre!*" he said.

As Cassandra and the Sheriff stared at him in silence, he removed the remote control from the pocket of his smoking jacket (odd name for the apparel of a man who didn't smoke, it occurred to me) and pressed a button.

The globe cover slid back into place, and he lay the remote control on top of the desk.

Plum turned and walked toward the entry hall.

"Don't leave the premises," he ordered. "I'll be back in less than an hour with a warrant."

"Warrant?" Max looked taken aback.

"To tear your goddam house apart," the Sheriff said.

"No need," Max told him instantly. "I confess. I *did* kill Harry Kendal."

My reaction was mixed. Surprise at his sudden, unexpected confession. Relief that it was over with.

After he spoke, a peal of thunder sounded, not too far away.

"How's that for timing?" Max inquired, pleased. "I even work the weather into my act."

The Sheriff looked repelled.

"Your *act?*" he said.

"Don't misunderstand," responded Max, his pleased expression gone. "I really did kill Harry Kendal."

Plum gestured toward the entry hall.

"In that case, we'll be on our way to town," he said.

Cassandra smiled, but Max looked disconcerted.

"No, no, please," he said. "That's not the plan." There *was* a plan, then! "The plan is to announce a murder to our good, staunch representative of law and order—that's you, Grover—then announce that he—you—will never ever—what's the phrase?—'pin the rap' on me, because he'll—you'll—never find the body."

Plum stared at him impassively.

"Let's get this straight," he said. "You're admitting to me—of your own free will—that you murdered Harry Kendal?"

"Of my own free will," said Max.

"And is your wife correct?" The Sheriff gestured toward Cassandra. "Is the body still in the house?"

Max's eyes lit up.

"Grover, *in this room,*" he said.

Why did you want me here, Max? Why? I wondered desolately.

Cassandra and Plum were looking at him in amazement.

"*However,*" Max continued, "if you take me in, I will—naturally—deny the murder. And without a signed confession, *and* without the *corpus delecti,* well . . ."

He gestured vaguely with his right hand.

"You just confessed in front of two witnesses," the Sheriff said.

"One of them my wife?" asked Max. "With me denying my confession? *Sans* corpse? The evidence not terribly incriminating?"

He waggled a chiding finger.

"*Grover,*" he scolded, parent to child.

The Sheriff was silent. Thinking. (I presume; can't prove it.)

"Take him in," Cassandra said. "*You* heard his confession. That's enough."

Max ignored her, addressing the Sheriff.

"I claim," he said, "that the worthless remains of Harry Kendal are in this room and that no one—*no one*—will ever be able to find them. Even though he may be no more distant from us than a few scant yards."

His smile was wicked. "Possibly *inches*," he said.

Despite the dreadful aspects of it all, I must confess that Max's challenge intrigued me. After all, wasn't he the product of my somewhat askew rearing?

I blinked (I think) as he made a sudden, broadly flourishing gesture with his right hand.

"I take it back!" he cried. "I didn't murder Harry Kendal! I *vanished* him!"

He smiled again. "In the parlance of the trade, that means I made him disappear, Grover." (I wished that he wouldn't keep calling Plum by his first name, and with such barely disguised disrespect.)

Max looked toward the fireplace.

"Perhaps I stuffed him up the chimney," he confided.

The Sheriff's head turned slightly—and involuntarily—toward the fireplace.

"Sheriff—" warned Cassandra.

"Or perhaps I dissected him into several hundred pieces, which are now distributed about the room in boxes, vases, urns, what have you."

"Delacorte—" said Plum.

"Or I may have disguised him as one or both of the easy chairs," Max interrupted. "Or had him pancaked under a steamroller so that he lies beneath that large rug over there."

"*Give it up,*" Cassandra told him.

"Or—" Max cut her off grandiosely—"I disassembled his integral atoms so that—even as I speak—he hovers in the air before our very eyes, an effluvium of cosmic dust."

He scowled theatrically.

"Or should I say cosmic *garbage?*" he amended.

"You're wasting my time, Delacorte," the Sheriff snarled.

Max made a face of boyish abashment. (*He can still do that?* I thought, amazed.) "Sorry," he murmured.

Plum turned to Cassandra.

"You think he's telling the truth?" he asked.

"*Gro-ver.*" Max sounded wounded. *You're getting in deeper and deeper, Son,* I thought.

Cassandra began to answer Plum, then hesitated, looking at Max as though she sought a confirmation in his face. Then she looked around the room as if searching for potential evidence.

"What think?" Max asked her.

She paid no attention to him, looking at the Sheriff.

"Yes, I do think he's telling the truth," she said. "I think he's gone so crazy that he's hidden Harry's body in this room . . . to torment me and to make a fool of you.

"To prove he's still *The Great Delacorte,* even though the world at large knows he isn't anymore."

She glared at Max, still speaking to the Sheriff. "Get your warrant," she said. "Tear the room apart."

"*Oh.* Come *on* now, Grover," Max said in a pouting voice. (*He still has* that *at his command as well!* I thought, incredulous.) "Don't do it that way. What fun is it to tear a room apart? That's no challenge."

He pointed at Plum, a look of provocation on his face.

"But to find it *yourself,*" he said, "*with your own wits.*"

He threw down the gauntlet.

"*Come* on, Grover," he said, "be a sport. How hard can it be to find one measly agent in a room this size?"

The Sheriff stared at Max. Remarkably, he seemed to be considering the offer.

"I have always dared my audience to find me out," Max said. (True; for both of us.) "I dare you now." He actually looked excited. "He's *here*, Grover," he promised. "I guarantee you."

The Sheriff remained quiet, regarding Max without expression.

"You wouldn't want to deprive my father of watching you meet the challenge, would you?" asked Max. "If you take me in, he has nothing."

My mind was split. *Max, I'd rather have nothing*, half of it said.

Go for it, Sonny! the other half was shouting. Shamefaced, but shouting.

"Sheriff, *get the warrant*," Cassandra said. She stared at him in disbelief.

"You aren't actually considering—"

She could not complete the statement.

"All right," said Plum. "As long as you realize that because of your confession to me, you're already in deep shit."

Max beamed.

"A predicament not unknown to me," he said.

"*Sheriff*—" Cassandra looked astounded.

Plum held up his right hand to stop her from speaking.

"I like a puzzle as well as the next man," he told her. "And it's a slow day at the office, nothing going on in town. They'll telephone if anything important comes up." He looked at Max.

"I accept your challenge," he said.

chapter 18

Max looked euphoric.

"Capital!" he cried.

His ebullience was not transferable. True, I did feel a sense of anticipation regarding what was about to happen. At the same time, however, the deep-set apprehension remained fixed in place. After all, he wasn't speaking about giving a show, he was speaking about murder.

"I'm going to find that body," Plum was telling him while I was ruminating. "And when I do—" his voice hardened "—I'll see to it personally that your ass is nailed to a cross."

Max looked at him with mocking admiration—but he must have felt at least a twinge of uneasiness.

Obviously, Cassandra still didn't believe that this was really taking place.

"I can take him in anytime, Mrs. Delacorte," Plum told her, "and I must say, I don't understand your objection. *You're* the one who said we should find the body first."

Touché, Grover, I thought.

Cassandra's teeth were bared. "All right," she said. "Play his stupid little game, then."

"I'll need your help," said Plum.

"Oh, now wait a mo," objected Max. "That's not fair. She knows this room better than you do."

"That's right," said Plum. His smile was thin and smug.

Cassandra looked at Max with sudden, vengeful pleasure.

"You think you're going to get away with this, don't you?" she said. "You know very well that this room is almost as strange to me as it is to him."

She pointed at Max, smiling now. Or was it *leering?*

"I'm not without means, however," she told him.

"Not without means at all!" cried Max.

He clapped his hands three times quickly as though announcing the commencement of a tourney.

"C'est merveilleux!" he cried. "What *fun* we're going to have!"

Thus the nightmare continued.

Visualize the scene, dear reader. (Assuming that anyone ever reads this.)

A wager had been made.

For money? Not so simple. Far more deadly and bizarre.

The location of a corpse.

Sheriff Plum and Cassandra Delacorte engaging in a challenge—he concedingly, she with resentful anger.

Puzzle?

Where was Harry Kendal's body in The Magic Room?

Remember the description now.

The room was twenty by thirty, high-ceilinged, many-windowed, including the picture window affording a view of the lake. Luxurious appointments, built-in bookshelves, a fieldstone fireplace and wall, the French desk, seven feet by four feet. The brass-and-teakwood bar, two easy chairs with end tables, the large antique globe, the display poster, the Egyptian burial case, the suit of armor, the casket, the guillotine; you remember all that, don't you?

Where would you begin to search for a corpse?

Play detective with Cassandra and Plum (unholy she and roly-poly he).

With the prior knowledge that no matter what solution you come up with, you will almost certainly be wrong.

Searching for a dead man.

My son's idea of "fun" (God help him).

What was he thinking as he crossed to the desk and sat on it, legs dangling while Cassandra and the Sheriff began their search?

Cassandra first examined the walls, of course; the obvious choice. She knew about one secret panel at least. Perhaps there were others she *didn't* know about; *I* didn't know about.

Plum, meantime, had moved to the Egyptian burial case and opened it.

"My wife already looked in there," Max told him with a smile.

"How do *you* know?" countered Plum. "You weren't here."

"Of course I was," Max said. He pointed. "In the suit of armor."

Plum grunted, checking the interior of the burial case anyway.

"Thoroughness," said Max. "I love it." He smiled genially. "Search every spot twice," he said. "Who knows what was missed the first time."

"You closed it up," says Plum. "I'm wondering why."

Max looked impressed; I knew he wasn't. "Good thinking, Grover," he said. "Wrong, but good."

Cassandra, by then, had looked behind the drapes and up

the fireplace; elementary steps. Now she was examining the chairs and end tables.

"You think he's in the end tables, love?" Max inquired, chuckling.

She glared at him. *"Be* amused," she said. "We'll find him."

Max bowed, smiling.

"Tell you what I'm going to do, Grover," he said to Plum.

"Sheriff," Plum reminded him.

"Yes, of course," Max said. "Tell you what I'm going to do, Sheriff. While you're searching, I'll describe some of my various escapes to entertain you. I'll even tell you how they work."

It is the measure of me, I confess, that I felt as much concern over that as I did about Harry Kendal's body.

Reveal how they work?

My effects? The ones I'd labored so long to develop and perfect?

Profanation.

"No loss," Max was saying, making it even worse for me. "I'm never going to use them again anyway." (Until that moment, I hadn't known the full extent of his hopelessness.)

"At any rate, they're too outdated, aren't they, Cassandra?" he said, his smile gone dead. "They're not *today."*

Cassandra only pressed her lips together. She would not respond.

"The Paper Bag Release!" cried Max. (*Don't do it, Son,* I thought.)

"A man-sized bag shaped like a giant fool's cap, a gummed seal at its top.

"I get inside, they seal it carefully and place a screen in front of it. Impossible to escape from without tearing the paper, you say?"

He cupped a hand behind his right ear as though anticipating a reply from them. They said nothing. I watched, heartsick.

"You *don't* say," Max went on. "Nonetheless, I'll tell you. (*Max!*)

"All I have to do is slit the bag along the top with a razor blade, conveniently hidden on my person.

"I pop out and make a *new* flap with gum and brush, also conveniently secreted on myself. The screen is removed—

"—*et voila!* The bag appears untouched, pristine.

"No one ever notices, you see, that the bag is two inches shorter. They don't look for that sort of thing."

Well, that trick's shot to hell now, I thought gloweringly.

The Sheriff had, while Max was speaking, left the mummy case behind and approached the lobby-display poster to look behind it.

Max snickered at that.

"He's not back there," he said. He stroked his chin reflectively. "Although I might have laminated him into the wood, I suppose."

The Sheriff touched the heart area of the poster figure.

"Someone's thrown a knife in here," he said.

"*Oh,*" responded Max in a voice of pseudo-awe. "I can see why you're the Sheriff of Medfield County, Grover."

Plum turned to him with a smile most icy and atypical, I thought.

"You think this is a grand game," he said.

"Completely grand," Max agreed.

"Well, what you don't know," the Sheriff said, "is that I'm going to nail you good."

Max extended his arms to each side, head dropped forward.

"To the cross, don't forget," he reminded Plum.

Then he lifted his head, grinning.

"The only fitting expiration for a saint," he said.

"A *snake*, you mean," Cassandra told him.

Max clucked and shook his head. "How disparaging," he muttered.

He put both palms down on the desk behind him and leaned back with a contented sigh. (I could not believe he was really contented, though.)

"Both of you are cold, you know," he said. "Virtually North Polish, if you want to know the truth."

"You really believe we're not going to find him, don't you?" Cassandra asked with a cold smile.

"You're not," he replied. "You especially, you're bordering on the frigid."

"Only with *you, lover*," she jeered.

That blow hit home. I saw it clearly as Max regarded her with malignance.

Then he turned from her to observe the Sheriff, who was at the fireplace, patting and running his hands over the stonework as though in search of another hidden panel.

Max watched with hooded eyes.

"Having a good time, Grover?" he asked.

The Sheriff did not reply; he continued what he was doing.

"The Iron Box Escape!" cried Max. (*Not again*, I thought, despairing. *How can he do this?*)

"The box is heavy—solid—riveted—the lid held down by bolts."

My stomach sank. He really *was* going to do it.

"I'm locked inside," he described. "The box is bolted shut. The good ol' screen is set in place for several minutes.

"I appear. The screen is withdrawn. The box is untouched, all bolts secure. Impossible, you say?"

I saw myself on stage performing the trick. To reveal its secret was unthinkable to me!

The Sheriff was by the picture window now, looking out at the lake.

"What's that out there?" he asked.

"*That* is a gazebo, Grover," Max told him.

"I don't mean that," said the Sheriff.

Cassandra joined him quickly. "Where?" she asked.

"*Grover*," scolded Max. "I *told* you; he's *in this room*."

"You told me a lot of things," Plum said in a deprecating voice. He pointed. "That thing out there. Like a mound."

Cassandra blew out a breath disgustedly. "It's just a pile of *stones*," she told the Sheriff.

"It was there before?" he asked.

"*Yes.*" She turned away.

"Good try, Grover," said Max. "My respect for you is mounting by the moment."

"Why don't you just shut up?" snapped Plum.

"Haven't finished my description of the Iron Box Escape," Max responded cheerfully. (*Oh, for* God's *sake, Max,* I thought.)

"The bolts I pushed out from the inside to have the nuts fastened to them *are not the original bolts,* you see; the ones examined by the judges. (*Damn you, Max!*)

"*These* bolts—secreted on my person, of course—have nuts on the *inside* of the box as well.

"I remove these inside nuts, push out the bolts, emerge, replace the original bolts with the expeditious use of string—that's the tricky part—*et voila!*"

Thanks a lot, Son, I thought. *Another pile of years and effort down the tube.*

While Max was talking, Plum had gone to check one of the built-in bookcases, running his fingers along the decorative moldings to see if anything occurred.

Occur it did.

As the Sheriff touched what appeared to be a scalloped

inlay on the molding, he (and I—and Cassandra, I imagine) heard a *clicking* sound.

The bookcase section hinged out by several inches.

"Ah," the Sheriff said.

chapter 19

Cassandra hurried over as the Sheriff tried to pull the bookcase open. "Now we're getting somewhere," he said.

Has the search already ended? I wondered.

Plum hissed as he broke a nail. "What *is* this, anyway?" he demanded.

"*Nothing*, Sheriff," said Max. He looked disturbed.

"*Nothing*, Max?" Cassandra goaded.

Seeing how the bookcase edge had sprung open several inches, she made a sound of vengeful satisfaction.

"*Now* we've got you," she said.

"I'm telling you, Sheriff, it's *nothing*," Max insisted.

"You *hear*?" Cassandra said. "He wouldn't say that if it was *really* nothing."

She looked at Plum.

"What were you doing?" she asked. "What did you touch?"

"This molding here," he answered, pointing.

Cassandra pressed her thumb along the molding designs. I felt my heartbeat thumping. *What was behind there?*

When Cassandra touched the scalloped inlay, she said excitedly, "It's going in!"

She looked at Max accusingly.

"Now we've got you, you son of a bitch," she said.

She held the scalloped inlay in and quietly, with well-oiled gears, the bookcase section started to revolve.

Cassandra and the Sheriff stepped back quickly, and I braced myself (as much as that was possible) for what I might see. Harry's corpse?

The bookcase section turned all the way around and stopped.

No Harry's corpse.

Books.

On the reverse side was another bookcase filled with them.

"What the hell *is* this?" the Sheriff asked.

Max smiled cutely (that smile again), a small shrug hunching up his shoulders.

"I told you it was nothing," he said. "I wish I could tell you that I'd fooled you, but I can't. It's just a protected place where I keep my more valuable books on magic."

So that's *where they are,* I thought. I'd noticed they were gone, but had assumed they were upstairs in Max's bedroom.

"For Christ's sake," muttered the Sheriff. He bit off the shredded nail's edge and spat it out in disgust.

"Good moment though, you must admit," said Max. (*It was,* I thought.)

He looked at Cassandra disdainfully.

"Better luck next time," he said.

He slid off the desk and walked to the bookcase, pressing in the scalloped inlay.

"Wait a second," said Cassandra.

Now what? I thought.

Max kept the inlay depressed with his thumb. Cassandra grabbed his arm and pulled it from the molding.

"I said *wait* a minute," she told him.

"What is it?" asked the Sheriff.

"Why is he so anxious to close it up?" she demanded.

Max made a weary sound.

"Give it up, Cassandra," he said. He depressed the scalloped inlay, and the bookcase started revolving again.

"Stop him, Sheriff," said Cassandra.

"Hold it," ordered Plum.

Max looked aggrieved. "For God's sake, Grover," he complained.

"I said *hold* it," said the Sheriff.

Max removed his thumb from the inlay.

"*I'd* like to know why you're so anxious to close it, too," said Plum.

"I *told* you," Max replied, a little testy now. "I like to keep a tidy household."

He jerked around, a look of anger flaring on his face as Cassandra shoved him aside and pressed at the scalloped inlay once again.

"Don't try to stop her," the Sheriff warned.

Motionless, Max watched as the bookcase closed all the way; then, as Cassandra kept the inlay depressed, it revolved once more. Again, the collection of Max's more valuable volumes of magic (my volumes, really) faced outward.

"Now," said Cassandra.

"*Leave it alone,*" Max told her. All geniality had vanished from his voice now; he was deadly serious. *Is this it?* I wondered.

Cassandra began to examine the bookcase.

Max moved to stop her.

Sheriff Plum stepped forward and restrained him.

I sat, lumplike, watching.

Max glared at the Sheriff. "This has nothing to do with Harry Ken—"

His voice broke off as Cassandra found a middle joint on the bookcase and began to pull open one side of it.

"Damn it!" said Max.

Both bookcase halves started to glide apart on rollers.

"*No!*" said Max. He tried to pull away from Plum, but couldn't.

He stared at the opening bookcase halves, his expression harried.

I couldn't see—or feel—my expression, but I wager it was no less distraught.

Cassandra hitched back with a gasp, and Plum's grip tightened reflexively on Max's arm.

I wanted to gasp, but couldn't.

What we were looking at was Adelaide Delacorte.

———————

Adelaide's back was turned to us, her hair and dress exactly as they looked in the painting above the fireplace.

"*Holy God,*" Plum muttered.

"God damn it!" Max snarled.

He jerked loose from the Sheriff's grip and moved to close the bookcase halves.

Too late.

Cassandra had already touched Adelaide's right shoulder. Adelaide began to turn. Slowly. Like a lifesized doll on a revolving base.

Which stopped.

We all stared at her face.

There was no face.

It was a faceless mannequin, wearing the dress and a wig. I felt a sense of dreadful pain for my son.

What had been exposed was a sanctuary to his wife, her

dresses and belongings lovingly displayed. Her jewelry. Her hats. Her books.

Total silence in TMR. Immobility.

Then Max, breath strained, said in a quiet (bating) voice, "Are you both satisfied now?"

Hands shaking, he began to close the bookcase again.

Cassandra grabbed his arm and jerked him around.

"You made a shrine to her?" she asked, infuriated. "A *shrine?*"

Max looked at her in blank surprise (as I did) as she shoved the bookcase halves apart again, so violently that the mannequin began to topple.

With a hollow cry, Max lunged for the figure to prevent its fall. He stood it up again.

Cassandra smiled now. It was not a wholesome smile.

"To the only woman you ever loved?" she asked.

"What's going on?" asked Plum. I would have asked the same question had I been able to speak.

"And *she* loved *you*, of course," Cassandra said. "Adored you. Worshiped you."

Max's face looked carved from stone. Again, he tried to close the bookcase halves to shut away what clearly was a shrine to Adelaide. Again, Cassandra stopped him.

It was impossible to believe that these two had ever loved each other, so rabid were their exchanged looks. I felt embarrassed to witness it. Plum seemed to feel the same.

"Time for a little truth, Max," said Cassandra. "Time to set things straight."

He started to speak. She cut him off.

"You never loved her for a second," she said.

He tensed. I tensed (I think). Plum tensed (I guess).

Cassandra's smile was ruthless.

"How *could* you love her," she said, *"when you loved yourself so much?"*

It seems accurate to say that Max was on the verge of leaping at her, probably to throttle her.

But somehow, he managed to hold back, his expression suddenly confused. *What does* that *mean?* I wondered.

"Oh, you *thought* you loved her," said Cassandra. "Why not? She never asked for a single thing."

Her face went hard. "Except a *baby,*" she added.

"Stop it," said Max. His voice was weak and vulnerable now.

"She spoke to me. You never knew that, did you?" said Cassandra. "During that engagement in New York. The night she died."

Her shiver seemed genuine enough.

"Or should I say the night she was killed?" she added.

"Stop it," Max commanded. He seemed to be losing control.

"Oh, no," Cassandra said through clenching teeth. "Not now. I'm sure the Sheriff will be fascinated by what I have to say. I'm sure your father would be too if he weren't a living *sponge.*" (*Gracias,* Cassandra.)

"I'm warning you," Max told her.

"Warn ahead," she said, defying him.

She turned to the Sheriff.

"My brother and I were performing at the same theater," she said. "I got to know Max's wife. She was pregnant. Oh, so happy to be carrying their first child."

"God damn you." Max's hands began to flex into fists.

"And oh, so exhausted because Max wouldn't let her rest," Cassandra continued, looking at Max as though daring him to try and stop her.

"She should have been in bed that night," she went on. "She was afraid she might miscarry. But did that mean a thing to Max? *No.* Not him. He didn't want the baby anyway."

"God damn you," Max broke in again.

"He couldn't stand the idea of Adelaide loving any other person in the world but him."

"*Stop it!*" shouted Max; it was the agonized protest of a man who knew he was hearing the truth. (A genuine shock to me.)

"You knew she shouldn't have been working that night!" Cassandra shouted back. "You didn't give a damn, though! You made her work, regardless! She miscalculated, had the accident—*and you're the one who killed her!*"

chapter 20

Max lunged at Cassandra, hands clutching for her throat.

Only Plum's alert move prevented him from succeeding.

"You didn't want a wife!" Cassandra raged at Max. "You wanted a slave! A smiling, bowing, scraping, worshiping slave! That's why Adelaide was your dream woman! Because, unlike me—"

She broke off breathlessly and turned away from him with a convulsive shudder.

"Let me go," Max told the Sheriff quietly.

"Not if you intend to harm your wife," said Plum.

Max replied, *"My wife is dead."*

My eyeballs shifted as I looked at Cassandra.

Not surprisingly, she was staring at Max with as much pain as venom.

Once again, I was compelled to sympathize with her. Whatever she'd done to harm Max—and it was considerable (she'd certainly gone beyond the bounds in her accusations)—she did not deserve his last remark. Good God, what a murk of hate and counter-hate befouled that room.

Enough to make a person ill.

Max had pulled loose from the Sheriff's relaxing grip and was now closing Adelaide's shrine, returning the bookcase to its original position.

He looked around in startlement as Cassandra suddenly lurched toward the fireplace.

She stopped in front of it and put a trembling hand across her eyes.

"Why did you rush over there?" the Sheriff asked.

She didn't answer.

"Mrs. Delacorte?"

"No reason," she said, struggling for composure.

Plum looked at her in disbelief. It was a wonder the man believed anything by then, there'd been so much deception since he'd arrived.

He moved to where she was standing.

"Is there something over here?" he probed. "A hiding place or something?"

"No," she muttered.

"Why did you come over here, then?" he asked.

"No reason!" She was still fighting to regain herself. "No reason at all," she said.

Clearly, Plum was not convinced. Who could blame him?

He ran his hands across the uneven surface of the field-stone wall above the fireplace. He looked carefully at the mantelpiece.

"If I knew where the body is," Cassandra said, "do you think I'd have been searching with you all this time?"

"*Frankly, I don't know*," the Sheriff said disgustedly. "I don't know whether to believe either one of you at this point."

Bravo, Grover, I thought gloomily. So far, this had been a little less than the happiest day of my life.

Plum could find nothing. With an irritated sound, he turned toward the entry hall.

"That's it," he said. "I'm not wasting any more time here."

"*I'll show you the body,*" said Cassandra.

Plum whirled to glare at her. "You just said you don't know where it is!" he cried.

"I *don't!*" she responded. "But I know how to find it without wasting any more time!"

She started toward Max, a vengeful look on her face. "I told you I'm not without means," she told him.

"Get away from me," he muttered.

"You'd best cooperate, Mister Delacorte," Plum said, "or I'll take you in right now."

Ambivalence flickered on my son's face, indecision; should he go or stay?

It wasn't much of a contest, as it turned out.

"What do you want?" he asked Cassandra.

Her answer was to grab his right wrist.

He jerked it free.

She grabbed the wrist again. Again, he pulled away.

"Make him do it, Sheriff," she said.

Plum looked agitated. *"Do what?"* he demanded.

"Lead me around the room while I'm holding his wrist."

The Sheriff scowled. *"Why?* What's that supposed to do?"

Her smile was cruel. The woman had a cruel smile, that was certain. Now I wondered just how much of what she'd said about Adelaide was true and how much concocted.

"When we reach the place where Harry Kendal's body is hidden," she told the Sheriff, "my husband's pulse beat will speed up."

So that was it; I should have known.

The Sheriff's scowl had not abated. "I'm tired of—" he started.

"Sheriff," said Cassandra. "I'm telling you. It will work."

The Sheriff sighed. He looked at Delacorte and nodded once.

With a smile equally cruel, Max extended his right hand and Cassandra grabbed the wrist again, squeezing as hard as she could. Max winced a little, then chuckled softly.

"Where to?" he inquired.

"Just lead me around the room," she said.

"Yes, ma'am," he replied.

He led her to the globe and stopped. "Here?" he asked.

"Go on," she muttered.

"Yes, ma'am."

He led her to the fireplace and then along the fieldstone wall. He gestured toward the fireplace with his left hand.

"Here?" he asked.

She gestured irritably for him to keep on moving.

"Yes, ma'am," he said.

"I'm not going to wait too long on this," the Sheriff told her.

"Hold on," she said.

Max led her to the desk and gestured toward it.

Cassandra grimaced and shook her head.

He led her to the suit of armor, stopped.

She shook her head.

He led her to the guillotine.

She shook her head.

With a bored sigh, he led her to the casket, stopped.

He waited, then began to move again.

She released his wrist, a look of sweet revenge on her face.

"I knew his pulse beat wouldn't change," she told the Sheriff. "He's too good at controlling it. He forgot his muscular reaction, though."

She is *clever*, I thought uneasily.

As she finished speaking, a roar of thunder sounded in the distance. Lightning flashed.

The storm was getting closer.

"Mrs. Delacorte," said Plum.

She pointed at the casket.

"He never keeps it closed," she said.

"But you can *see inside*," Plum told her.

Cassandra's pointing finger shifted toward the lower portion of the casket.

"Not down there," she said.

Max spluttered with contemptuous amusement. His distress at the uncovering of his shrine to Adelaide seemed ended now; he had his equanimity back.

"You can't be serious," he said.

He looked at Plum.

"I could conceal the body in a dozen different places, Grover," he said. *"But in a casket right in front of you?"*

He directed a hooded-eyed smile at Cassandra.

"Nom de Dieu, ma petite," he said.

His voice grew harsh.

"I'm referring to the size of your brain, of course," he added.

Cassandra was trying in vain to open the casket.

"Make him unlock it," she said to Plum.

Plum looked at Max as though he really didn't see the point in this but felt compelled to try it anyway.

"You have the key, Mister Delacorte?" he asked.

"Ah, it's *Mister* Delacorte again," said Max. "Things are picking up."

"Will you just unlock it, please," Plum told him.

"Sheriff," Max explained, "that casket is my final resting-place-to-be. It has a deep significance—"

Plum didn't let him finish.

"If you force me to get a warrant," he said, "I swear to God I'll break it open with an axe."

"You-will-not," said Max, offended.

Even so, he hesitated for several moments more before removing a key from the right-hand pocket of his smoking jacket and tossing it to Plum, who, startled, was barely able to snatch it from the air.

Was this *it, then?* I wondered. Trepidation held me tight.

Cassandra edged closer to the casket.

"Anxious to view your lover's remains?" asked Max.

The look she gave him was now as apprehensive as malign. I could not believe that he could sound so casual if this was really *it.* Unless he had surrendered inwardly already.

They watched (I watched) as the Sheriff unlocked the casket's upper lid and opened it.

Reaching in, Plum lifted out the partial replica of Max and set it on the floor, then rejoined Cassandra, who was looking down into the casket.

Their reaction made it obvious that they were seeing nothing.

Max chuckled again. "I *told* you," he said.

Moving to the Sheriff, he removed the key from Plum's fingers and dropped it back into his pocket.

Cassandra had backed off, frowning, but the Sheriff still looked down into the interior of the casket.

Max looked inside with him.

"Satisfied?" he asked.

Does he feel as sick inside as I do? I wondered. I'm sure he did.

The Sheriff remained silent, peering into the casket.

"All right if I put my quarter-duplicate back in?" asked Max.

Plum did not respond. He reached down into the casket, feeling at the padding.

"Grover?" Max put his hand on the Sheriff's shoulder. Plum shook it off.

Abruptly then, he raised the bottom lid of the casket,

hinging it aside. He poked at the interior padding once again. *What is he looking for?* I wondered.

Max wondered, too.

"What are you *doing?*" he asked, his tone a rather obvious attempt to sound casually curious.

Still the Sheriff didn't speak. He began to press both hands against the padding now. He was on to something, I could see.

Also seeing it, Cassandra returned. "What is it?" she asked.

"Sheriff?" Max inquired.

Plum remained quiet, pressing harder at the inside padding of the casket, poking it and plucking at it.

The approaching thunder rumble sounded ominous to me. Like a drumroll prior to some explosive finale.

Now Plum reached into his right-hand trouser pocket and removed a folding knife.

"What are you doing?" Max asked quickly.

Plum opened the knife.

"What are you doing?" Max repeated, now more urgently.

Plum reached into the casket, the open knife in his right hand.

Max grabbed his arm. "You aren't going to do this," he declared.

"Let go of me," Plum said. His tone was threatening.

Max swallowed and withdrew his hand. "You'll regret this," he said.

Ignoring him, Plum began to cut away the padding on the bottom of the casket.

"You're going to pay for this," Max told him.

Cassandra watched in silence as the Sheriff hacked at the casket padding, pulling it up in handfuls.

Suddenly, Cassandra looked inside the casket in shock.

"Oh, my God," she murmured.

What is it? cried my mind.

The Sheriff was pulling something up from an apparent cavity in the bottom of the casket.

Something heavy.

Oh, no, Max, no, I thought.

The Sheriff hauled up what appeared to be a cloth sack.

Cassandra (and I) choked on breath as the Sheriff yanked the heavy bag up higher and it toppled from the casket, landing on the floor with a soggy thump.

Dripping blood.

chapter 21

Cassandra made a sickened noise; somewhere in my vegetated bowels, I did alike.

The Sheriff swallowed, throat dry.

Bracing himself, he reached down with both hands and cut open the sack with his knife.

He pulled apart the edges.

And cried out hoarsely—simultaneously with Cassandra—as a giant paper moth flew upward from inside the sack, flapped around in erratic circles, then performed an abrupt nosedive to the floor.

"I told you you'd regret it," Max reminded the Sheriff.

What was that hollow sound inside my chest? Could it have been a chuckle? I felt like chuckling. From relief. From (damn my magicianly hide!) appreciation and delight at a trick well done.

"The weight is dirt," Max told them. "The blood is fake."

Both looked at him with virtually the same expression—one of incredulous revulsion.

"I also told you it was my casket," Max continued

blithely. "It *is.* I had a few small gimmicks put in, that's all. To entertain the audience at my funeral. Why let them sit there morosely when I can do a postmortem performance?"

"Morosely?" Cassandra responded, glaring at him. "Don't you mean *joyously?*"

"Only you," said Max.

To their surprise (and mine, need I add?) he started climbing into the casket.

"Let me demonstrate," he said. He closed the lower lid, locking it into place.

"You'll get a boot out of this, Grover," he told the Sheriff.

He lay back against the padding, his head on the sewn-in pillow.

"I'm in my casket, see?" he said. "Laid out in my finest bib and tucker, hair combed, beard trimmed, teeth all brushed; why not?

"The service is near concluded. Get the picture? Lights are dimmed. All heads are lowered reverently."

"Murderer!" Cassandra snarled.

Lunging at the casket, she slammed shut the upper lid, locking it. Max cried out. Max's father felt a surge of dread.

Cassandra seemed to be uncertain as to whether she felt shock or elation. She trembled visibly as she watched Plum attempt to open the casket.

"You bitch!" screamed Max. His voice was muffled.

"Where's the key?" the Sheriff asked him loudly.

"In my *pocket,* you idiot!" shrieked Max, furious and terrified at the same time.

Oh, my God, she's done him in, I thought.

Plum was staring blankly at the casket.

He looked at Cassandra, stunned, as she emitted a sound of half-mad pleasure.

"I'm going to *smother* in here!" Max shouted.

"Your breath is steaming up the faceplate, darling," Cassandra said, smiling.

"Mrs. *Delacorte*," said Plum, aghast.

"I hope his death is *slow*," she said.

Which concluded my appraisal of Cassandra Delacorte.

Not a positive one.

The Sheriff was staring at her as though he couldn't believe what he'd heard.

I stared at her with no difficulty at all in believing what I'd heard.

Max started pounding on the inside of the lid (unbreakable glass), screaming with enraged terror.

The Sheriff looked around, gaze settling on the trophy board above the mantelpiece.

Running there, he grabbed the African spear.

Seeing this, Cassandra quickly levered down the casket to a horizontal position.

"What are you doing?" Max shouted; he sounded deranged now.

When the Sheriff started to return with the spear, Cassandra pushed the rolling-casket base away from him.

"You mustn't touch his casket, Sheriff," she said breathlessly. "You heard him."

It was a manic chase, my friends. A farce enacted in a madhouse.

Visualize: Cassandra Delacorte shoving the casket around the room (no Magic Room now; rather, an insane asylum), a look of unhinged amusement on her face.

Max inside, howling, pounding.

Plum—the Kikuyu spear clutched tightly in his right hand—gasping, "Mrs. Delacorte!"

And Potato Familias ensconced, unmoving, in his wheelchair, watching like the helpless tuber he was.

"Mrs. Delacorte!" Plum cried again.

"No, no, it's his final resting place!" she protested. She *was* insane; I note this in retrospect.

A frenetic giggle pulled back her lips as she yawed the

casket around the guillotine, turning so fast that it "did a wheelie," as they say.

"Damn it!" cried the Sheriff.

He put on a burst of speed and managed to catch up to her, forcing her to stop.

Immediately, she backed off, panting.

Plum attempted to pry the spearhead under the lid.

Max's pounding was weaker now. He sobbed with dread.

"Get me out of here!" he begged. "For Christ's sake, get me out of here!"

The glass plate, I could see now, was completely steamed up by his breath.

"Damn!" Plum was grimacing angrily. He couldn't seem to force the spear in to open the lid.

I wanted to close my eyes. The sight was unnerving me; and my nerves were half dead, remember.

Plum struggled harder. Finally, he forced the point in and started pulling down on the shaft.

Which promptly broke.

"*Oh,*" Cassandra said, her tone nine steps below sincerity. "*Drat.*"

She smiled benignly at the casket. "Sorry, Max," she said.

"You bitch!" he shrieked.

Cassandra clucked and shook her head. "How disparaging," she said, leaning across the casket as Sheriff Plum ran back toward the fireplace.

"Now you'll pay for killing Harry," she said. "Whether we find him or not."

"*Damn* you!" cried my son, his voice sounding faint.

The Sheriff snatched the Spanish pike from the trophy board and started running back, gasping for breath.

"He's going to try the pike now, Max," Cassandra told my son. "If that doesn't work, we'll send out for some dynamite."

"Look out," said Plum.

Cassandra jumped aside as the Sheriff reached the casket, brandishing the pike to drive it at the casket lock.

"Avaunt!" cried Max.

My heart jumped (it was nice to have *something* that could jump) as the casket side sprang open and my son stood up, arms raised to halt the Sheriff's move.

"Don't do it!" he ordered.

They stared at him in shock; while my body considered indulging in a second stroke.

Max gestured toward the casket.

"It is, of course, an apparatus," he confessed. "An interior release making possible solid-through-solid penetration."

He looked at Cassandra darkly.

"Although this *person* didn't know that," he said.

He looked over at me. "Had the apparatus built by Needlebaum," he told me. "He's still the best, at eighty-four."

His expression softened as he saw (or sensed) my distress. He came over to me.

"I know, I've made you suffer again," he said. "I regret that, *Padre*, but I wanted you to see these things and not be shut away from them. This is still your home."

He laid his hand on my right shoulder and squeezed it. *Dear, oh, dear,* my muddled brain remarked. My emotions were dangling at the end of a yo-yo, moving up and down, out and in, in circles, winging, spinning, penduluming.

Turning, Max went back to Cassandra and Plum. (Good name for a vaudeville team, it occurred to me.) They stared at him, still—I took it—recovering from the shock of his unexpected appearance.

He chuckled at their expressions.

"Now I ask you," he said. "Would I have a real casket in my father's home? Do I strike you as the morbid type?"

He addressed the Sheriff.

"As you know," he said, "—or maybe not—a magician always provides an alternative ending to an illusion in the event something goes wrong."

Again, the icy look at Cassandra.

"Like some *person* slamming down the lid of one's casket, locking one inside with the key."

He smiled at her, the smile as icily malignant as the look had been.

"Well, it was worth it," he declared. "Now I know exactly where your head is at."

He made a sound of derisive amusement.

"Even if you don't know where Harry's is at," he said.

The Sheriff finally found his voice; the casket effect seemed to have rendered him temporarily speechless.

"You let us think that you were suffocating just to play a *trick* on us?" he asked, appalled.

"*Just to play a trick?*" echoed Max. "*Sang-de-boeuf*, what greater achievement *is* there?"

His expression hardened suddenly.

"Speaking of that," he went on, "you've been fooled completely, Sheriff. Utterly deceived.

"Harry Kendal isn't here. He left at twelve-fifteen. I *have* been playing a game with you. Not a stupid game, as this *person* described it, but a game nonetheless."

The Sheriff's expression was as hard as Max's now, his lips pressed together so tightly they were barely visible.

"If you'd like to call a lawyer, Mister Delacorte," he said, "I advise you to do it now. I'm taking you in."

Max looked taken aback. "But I just told you—" he began.

The Sheriff cut him off. "I know what you told me," he said.

He moved to the chair in which Harry had been sitting and reaching into the narrow opening beneath it, slid out an attaché case.

"I also know that this is here," he said.

He pointed to the monogram. "And that H.K. doesn't stand for Maximilian Delacorte."

My son looked blank. He'd overlooked *that?*

"How long have you known it was there?" he asked.

Plum's smile was arctic.

"*I can play a game too*, Mister Delacorte," he said.

chapter 22

Max mumbled, *"Nom de Dieu."*

He nodded, impressed, then said, "I don't suppose I could convince you that Harry left the case behind, could I?"

"I don't suppose you could," said Plum coldly.

"Hmm." Max looked uncertain. *He seems to have lost focus,* I thought. "I appear to be at a loss here," he said. "Although I might remind you that you haven't found a body yet."

Weak, Max, weak. The thought oppressed me.

Throughout this brief exchange, Cassandra had been gazing fixedly at Max, a look of bewilderment on her face. Clearly she had little notion of what was going on at the moment. Neither did I.

Sheriff Plum reached into his back pocket and removed a pair of handcuffs.

My son protested. "Oh now, wait a moment—"

Plum did not reply. Walking over to Max, he tucked the attaché case under his left arm and deftly snapped the cuffs into place around Max's wrists.

"I don't usually put these on people," he said. "It humiliates them too much."

Max recognized the dig and nodded once in mute appreciation. *Is it over now?* I wondered. What, in fact, had actually been accomplished here?

As Cassandra (and I) watched in confusion, the Sheriff started to lead Max toward the entry hall, holding the attaché case with his left hand.

"I'll be back with a warrant, Mrs. Delacorte," he told her.

He glanced at Max in disgust. "At which time, we will tear this room apart until we find the body. And if the body isn't here, we'll tear the goddam house apart."

"Grover, I *told* you it was in this room," said Max. *Is he already backing down?* I thought.

The Sheriff didn't respond.

"Wait a second," said my son as though a bulb had just been switched on in his brain. "It's the *body* you want?"

Plum's face tightened—as did his grip on Max's arm, making my son wince.

"Well," said my son, "if *that's* all you want—"

He made a sudden twisting movement, and before Plum knew what was happening, he was staring down the barrel of his own pistol, which Max had, with great celerity, jerked from the Sheriff's holster. (Despite everything, I had to admire Max's still-impressive dexterity.)

Plum held out his right hand.

"Hand it over, Delacorte," he said.

Max edged back. "You said you wanted the body," he responded.

"Delacorte." The Sheriff advanced a step.

Froze in his tracks as Max thrust out the pistol threateningly.

"What have I got to lose, Grover?" Max asked. (Was it my imagination, or was there a crazed sound in his voice?) "Can they execute me twice for two murders?"

Cassandra shrank away from him as he passed nearby—
—backing toward the Egyptian burial case.

"You made me nervous before, looking at it a second time," he said to Plum. "I thought for sure you'd find out how the reversal gimmick works."

He pressed the side of the burial case, his voice suddenly becoming that of *The Great Delacorte* addressing an audience.

"I sense a gathering of forces, my friends," he said. "Can you feel it?"

Thunder crashed in the distance. (*By God, he really* does *work the weather into his act!* I thought.) The Magic Room was gloomy with shadows by now.

The Sheriff and Cassandra watched him, mute and motionless. (I was M&M too, of course.)

"Very close now," said *The Great Delacorte*. "Can you *feel* it? Feel the presence? The still, cold presence . . . of the *dead?*"

He flung open the cover of the burial case.

Cassandra screamed. The Sheriff gasped. I almost filled my pants.

Harry looked exactly as he had in the globe, features gray in death, a dark, blood-clotted gash across his throat.

"*Behold your lover!*" cried *The Great Delacorte*.

Max scowled.

"And the crummiest agent I ever had," he added pettishly.

Oh, Max, I thought. *Oh, Son.*

The scene was frozen; a tableau: Max immobile, the pistol in his hand; Cassandra and the Sheriff looking toward the burial case, their features and bodies as unmoving as stone; me immobile (same old thing), my heartbeat thudding, my heart breaking for my son's atrocity.

Harry staring, throat cut, dead.

"Don't you want to take a closer look, Cassandra?" asked her husband.

She averted her face with a choking sob.

"Take a closer look, Cassandra," Max urged.

"Give me the pistol, Delacorte," the Sheriff told him.

He twitched back as Max thrust out his arm, pointing the pistol at him.

"Take a closer look, Cassandra," Max ordered.

The Sheriff swallowed with some effort. With an attempt at professional demeanor, he suggested, "Better do as he says, Mrs. Delacorte."

"Good advice, Grover," my son complimented him. "You're a pip of a lawman, has anyone ever told you that before?"

The Sheriff did not reply. (I didn't blame him.) He edged slowly toward the burial case as Cassandra approached it, gaze averted.

Max backed off several paces, eyeing them with guarded care. And all I could think was: *Why did you want me here, Son? To see* this?

The Sheriff stopped, peering closely at Harry's face, grimacing at the sight—the bluish lips; the glassy, staring eyes; the deep, blood-rimmed incision across his throat.

Then he cocked his head, a look of curiosity on his face.

"Can I—" He gestured toward the body.

"Be my guest," said Max.

The Sheriff took a few steps closer to the burial case and laid the palm of his right hand against Harry's gray cheek. *What's he doing?* I wondered.

Noting the Sheriff's movement, Cassandra raised her eyes, emitting a sound of sickened pain at the sight of Harry's face.

She tensed as the Sheriff reached up to the top of Harry's head and took hold of his hair.

"What are you doing?" she asked in a faint voice. *What are you doing?* I thought.

He did not respond, but started to tug upward at Harry's hair.

Cassandra looked aghast. "What are you doing?" she demanded again, this time in a breaking voice.

"We are about to surprise you, my friends," said Max, once more *The Great Delacorte* addressing his audience. "Are you ready? Prepare yourselves. *Here it comes!*"

Plum pulled up hard at Harry's hair.

With a sound of revolted anger, Cassandra moved to stop him.

Suddenly, a skintight rubber mask—fastened loosely at the back—tore free from Harry's head, revealing him gagged but quite alive, making tiny sounds of protest—which the Sheriff had heard, I assumed.

Cassandra cried out with intense relief.

"Restoration, my friends!" cried *The Great Delacorte.*

He held out the pistol.

"Here's your weapon, Grover," he said.

Plum turned, regarding Max with a blank expression.

Max made a rapid, blurring movement with his hands and held out the handcuffs to Plum.

"And your little manacles, too," he said, sounding like the Witch of the North.

He looked at me.

"Sorry again, *Padre,*" he said. "Hope it wasn't too much of a shock."

Just how much do you think this battered old heart of mine can take, Son? I thought. I was relieved that he wasn't a murderer. Resentful that he'd forced me over the jump like that.

■▬▭

Cassandra, crying, was removing Harry's gag by then.

"You're alive," she said, incredulous. "*Alive.*"

"Yes, isn't that a nice surprise?" said Max. "A lot more *bedding* to be savored now."

She didn't even look at him.

The Sheriff took the pistol and the handcuffs from him.

"Never, in the fifty-four years of my life," he said, "have I ever met anyone as sick as you."

"Probably not," my son agreed; and so, unhappily, did I. Max was not amused, though. It was simply a statement of fact as he (and I) saw it.

"I'd like to shoot you dead where you stand," said Plum in a most unSheriffly way.

"Oh, now you're talking," said Max, nodding with somber approval. "That would be a lovely, charitable thing to do. Relieve me of my rapidly dwindling *raison d'être*. Please do. I encourage it."

He pressed the tip of his right index finger to the heart area of his chest.

"*Right here,*" he said.

"Don't tempt me," said the Sheriff, surprising me again.

Harry's gag was off now. Raging, he exploded. "If you won't do it, I will! Just give me the fucking gun!"

"Ah," said Max, "our sweet-tongued Harry is among us once again."

"You son of a bitch!" shrilled Harry. "You lousy, stinking, heartless son of—"

"*Enough!*" Max roared, shutting Harry up, causing him to twitch in startlement. "Be grateful that I didn't fire a *real* pistol ball into your heart! That the Scotch was merely drugged! It would have been a simple matter to dispose of you, and I have every reason in the world to wish you dead! So, *shut up.* Just don't push your luck! I'm not—"

He broke off with a groan of angry despair.

"Oh, what's the use?" he said. "Why bother? *What's the point in going on?*"

He looked around in restless torment, as though searching for some quick and simple exit from this life.

Abruptly then, with a sudden, crazed look on his face, he lurched toward the guillotine and, kneeling quickly, thrust his head through the lunette, under the glinting blade. *No,* I thought.

"All right, Harry. *Pal,*" he said, his tone both hating and anguished at once. "Here's your opportunity. Your big chance. To get revenge, get even. Get Cassandra. Get *everything.*"

Harry's bindings had been untied by Cassandra now. He started toward Max, trembling with fury.

"You think I couldn't do it, you bastard?" he snarled ferociously. "You think, if the damn thing was real, I wouldn't do it in a second?"

"But it *is* real, Harry," said my son. A chill around my heart again.

"Sure it is, you prick," snapped Harry.

"Harry, get away from there," Cassandra said. *My God, it isn't real, is it?* I thought in sudden dread.

"*Do* it, Harry," Max urged him. "Go *ahead*—to coin a phrase."

"You miserable son of a bitch," said Harry.

He reached for the lever.

"Harry, no!" Cassandra cried. *No!* my mind cried with her.

Too late. Harry was jerking down the wooden lever, the wide blade was hurtling downward, and Cassandra was screaming.

As Max's head dropped heavily into the basket.

chapter 23

O h, my good God," muttered Plum.

Harry resembled a man who had just been kicked in the testes by a mule.

He turned to Cassandra, barely able to speak.

"*It's not a trick?*" he murmured shakily.

"I told you to get away from there!" she cried.

Harry was staggered; petrified.

"I thought *everything* in this room was a trick," he whimpered.

"Well, you were wrong!" she responded.

Jabber away, I thought in agony. *Meantime, my son has been decapitated.*

Harry turned and stumbled toward the bar, avoiding the sight—as they all did but me—of Max's motionless body lying on the trestle of the guillotine.

Reaching the bar, he picked up the bottle of Scotch and unscrewed its cap.

He started to pour himself a glassful, then abruptly became conscious of what he was doing and lost his grip on the bottle, which clattered into the sink but didn't break; the noise made all of us twitch.

"Jesus, I was pouring Scotch," he said. He stared at them, a broken man. "Jesus Christ Almighty. *Scotch.*"

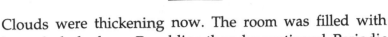

Clouds were thickening now. The room was filled with long, dark shadows. Rumbling thunder continued. Periodic lightning flashes bleached the sky, making me blink. (I think . . . but then, I don't really know if I twitched either.)

Harry had picked up a new bottle of brandy and was opening it.

As he did, the Sheriff began to edge toward the guillotine, features set, bracing himself for the sight of Max's severed head (perhaps twitching, the awful image presented itself) in the basket. *Oh, God, please let it be an effect,* I begged. *Not a real guillotine.*

Harry poured himself a glass of brandy and lifted it toward his lips with a palsied hand.

As Cassandra cried out hoarsely, the glass jerked in his grip and he flung the brandy across his shirtfront.

The Sheriff had lurched back with a hiss of astonishment.

I felt rage and relief (and bowel stress) simultaneously.

Max had just stood up.

His head, need I add, intact.

"You were quite correct 'old friend,' " he said to Harry, smiling thinly. "Everything in this room *is* a trick."

His soft laugh was a chilling one. It faded as he looked at me.

"*Mea culpa* once again, *Padre,*" he said. "I simply couldn't resist one more go at him. After all, remember what he did . . . not only to me, but to you."

I didn't know if that was adequate motivation for what he'd done to Harry, but I said nothing. (As per usual.)

Harry seemed beyond rage now, so traumatized by

everything he'd experienced that he was unable to even address my son.

Instead, he turned to Cassandra.

"Get your things," he said in a strained voice.

Cassandra started. "What?"

Harry grimaced, his teeth on edge.

"I presume you aren't planning to stay here with this maniac," he said.

Cassandra looked caught off guard (I wondered why.) "I'll be all right," she said.

"All *right?*" Harry gaped at her, incredulous. "The man is insane!"

Yes, I think he may have been.

Cassandra tried to answer Harry, but he cut her off, his voice agitated.

"You can't possibly intend to stay here with him after what he's done!" he cried.

"I agree with him," the Sheriff broke in.

"I—" Cassandra looked confused. I didn't understand it; *then.*

"Come on, get your things," Harry interrupted. "You can't stay here. That would be *ridiculous.*"

All of us were looking at Cassandra now. Was Max as perplexed by her reluctance? Was Plum?

"Come *on,* babe," Harry insisted. "You know you have to leave."

"I really think you'd better, Mrs. Delacorte," the Sheriff told her. Sheriffly again.

"All right." She turned toward the entry hall.

"*Wait,*" said Max.

She turned and looked back at him.

He sighed, surrendering.

"All right," he said. "I give up. I'll do the Vegas show exactly as you want."

Somehow, all the shocks I'd been exposed to in the previous hour diminished before the shock of this.

After all that, he was actually selling out the act?

"We'll talk about updating the set," he was continuing, twisting this new knife in my heart. "We'll simply—"

He broke off suddenly with a sound suspiciously like the birth of a sob.

Turning away, he walked to the picture window overlooking the lake, his movements infirm, those of a defeated old man. And that I hated to see.

Standing before the window, he shuddered with a deep breath.

"Just don't leave me," he said. "Try to understand."

He rubbed his eyes slowly, tiredly.

"I know I can't undo this afternoon," he said. "But blame it on the weakness of a man who sees his life disintegrating."

He turned back, his expression one of total pleading. "Please," he said. *"I need your help."*

Son, I thought, despairing. *I would almost rather that you murder than lie down and die like this.*

Cassandra was looking at him, no less confused than Harry or, I thought, the Sheriff. She couldn't seem to deal with this new perplexity.

Neither could she walk away from it.

"All right," she finally said, her voice extremely quiet.

Incredible, I thought. *They're going to be together again?*

Harry stared at her with unbelieving eyes.

"You're *staying?"* he asked.

"I'll be fine," she responded. (*Madness!* I thought.)

She looked at the Sheriff.

"You'll be keeping an eye on him, won't you?" she asked.

The Sheriff didn't answer. (I could well believe it.) He looked at Max, then at her again, as though attempting (with obviously limited means) to penetrate this new enigma: Cassandra, prepared to remain with her clearly demented husband after everything he'd done to her and Harry—and to the Sheriff, for that matter—in the past hour or so.

"For God's sake—" Harry started.

"Harry, I'll be fine," she cut him off.

"You *believe* him?" he asked. "You actually *believe* the son of a bitch?"

She didn't answer that; she probably couldn't.

Harry made a sound of total incredulity. "Jesus Christ," he said.

He gestured with both hands, giving up.

"Okay," he said, his mild tone obviously belying the sense of utter disgust he felt. "Fine. To hell with it. *Stay* with him!"

Seeing his attaché case still in Plum's left hand, he took it from the Sheriff and looked around.

"Where's my hat?" he asked.

Immediately, he made a sound of angry indifference. "*Fuck* it," he said.

He turned to give Cassandra a good-bye kiss.

She turned away and walked to the picture window. "Good-bye, Harry," she said.

And she'd been so upset by his disappearance and probable murder, I thought, dumbfounded. *What in the merry Hell is going on?*

Harry had stopped in his tracks to stare at her, no doubt equally dumbfounded by her contradictory behavior.

He stared at her for several moments, then turned abruptly for the entry hall.

"Let me out of this frigging nuthouse," he muttered.

Moving, he glanced at Cassandra.

"So long, *babe*." He directed a cold farewell at her.

"I'll mail you your hat," Max told him.

"*Don't bother*," Harry responded.

The Sheriff spoke quickly.

"Are you going to press charges, Mr. Kendal?" he asked.

Harry stopped and looked around. He gazed at Max, and I could tell that he was sorely tempted.

Then he gestured with a scowl.

"No, let him have his stupid little victory," he said. "It's all he'll have to live on for the rest of his loser life."

He glared at Max.

"You're nothing to me anymore," he said. "Not a client. Not a friend. Not even a human being. We're quits. *Finished.*"

Max's smile was nearly imperceptible.

"We were finished years ago," he said.

Harry directed a final, glacial look at him, then exited.

They stood motionless and silent as his footsteps moved across the entry hall. The front door opened, shut.

Harry Kendal was gone.

And then there were three.

Four, if you (compassionately) include Mr. Cauliflower.

Harry, we discovered later, walked to the highway, found a phone booth, and called for a taxi.

The Sheriff turned to Max.

"Before I go," he said, "I want you to know that your wife is right—

"I *am* going to keep an eye on you from now on.

"If I wanted to, I could take you in now for what you've done.

"But I'd rather you were on the outside, knowing that I'm watching you, whatever you do."

His expression altered to one of contempt.

"If you took pleasure in fooling me, you take your pleasures pretty cheaply," he continued.

"I'm the Sheriff of a small New England county. You're a professional magician.

"Do you really think it was some grand accomplishment to make your magic work on me?

"If you do, if that's really how you earn your sense of pride, you have no *real* pride at all that I can see."

He smiled at Max; a faint, derisive smile.

"Good-bye, *Great Delacorte*," he said.

He changed his mind.

"No, not good-bye," he said. The derision turned to animosity. *"Until we meet again,"* he finished.

Max could only lower his head, the criticism uncontested.

I was glad he had the decency to do that, anyway.

The Sheriff gave Cassandra one more extended, searching look.

Then he turned and walked toward the doorway.

His footsteps moved across the entry hall.

The front door opened, closed.

And then there were two.

chapter 24

I say there were two now. Of course, there were three, but you may just as well consider me invisible in this account. Except for an occasional apology from my son, I pretty much *was* invisible. Fortuitous, I suppose. If it hadn't been for my ignored presence, none of this would have ever been recorded.

Where were we?

Max and Cassandra standing motionless, the Sheriff having just departed; me sitting motionless, as usual.

It was Cassandra who finally spoke.

"I'm sure they're gone," she said.

Not exactly what I might have expected to hear.

Max did not reply but moved to the bar with a look of undisguised hostility on his face.

Walking to one of the easy chairs, Cassandra sank down on it with a weary groan and slipped off her shoes.

Sighing, she began to wiggle her toes.

At the bar, Max had picked up the fallen bottle of Scotch and begun pouring the remainder of its contents into the sink, flushing it down with water from the faucet. He dropped the empty bottle into the wastebasket.

I watched him, curious, as he opened a cabinet door above the bar, removed a bottle of private-stock brandy, unsealed and thumbed off its cork, then poured some into a snifter.

He downed it with a swallow; sighed.

Poured himself a second drink and sipped it slowly.

"Oh, yes," he said, pleased.

What's going on? I wondered.

I was not too long in finding out.

Cassandra chuckled.

"I thought I'd have a stroke when he decided to kiss me good-bye," she said.

"You made precious little effort not to leave with him," Max countered.

What was going on?

"He caught me off guard, what can I say?" said Cassandra.

She chuckled again.

"That would have been priceless, wouldn't it?" she asked.

She threw back her head with a laugh.

"Especially at bedtime."

Her amusement vanished abruptly, and she looked at Max with bleak distaste. My mind was churning, trying to understand what was happening.

"You prevented my departure most convincingly," she said. "I almost believed you."

Max finished his second drink of brandy, poured himself a third.

He walked over to the easy chair, looking at Cassandra with distaste.

"A wonderful performance," he said scornfully. "Absolutely wonderful."

Performance?

"What do you want from me?" Cassandra asked.

"Nothing I received, that's certain," Max responded.

He pointed across the room. "What in the bleeding *hell* was that performance over there supposed to mean?" he asked. "Who told you to show Adelaide's shrine to that *clod?*"

His features stiffened with fury.

"And how the hell did you know it was there in the first place?" he demanded.

"I *didn't.*" Her voice was tense. "I was only playing the game—*as per instructions.*"

What the hell are they talking about? My brain was totally muddled now.

"Almost *ruining* the game, you mean!" Max was ranting.

He pointed toward the fireplace.

"Bad enough that fool almost stumbled onto the truth by himself! You had to go over there and arouse his suspicion a *second* time! Were you *insane?*"

Her expression was now as hard as his. "Just angry," she muttered.

"I see." He regarded her, disgusted. "Well, it's fortunate for you your little *snit* didn't give it all away. Otherwise, you'd be in jail by nightfall."

My mind howled: *What is going on?!*

Max sank down on the other easy chair; he looked exhausted. He took another sip of brandy.

"God, I needed this," he said.

He sighed heavily, then managed a contemptuous smile.

"I can't believe that idiot Sheriff finally found the attaché case I'd hidden so ineptly," he said. "I thought we'd be here for a week before he did."

He sighed again, rubbing his eyes.

"However, as he said," he went on, "it was no grand accomplishment to fool him. I felt rather sorry for him, actually. He tried his futile best."

By then, my mind had fallen back in submission. Was it the stroke's aftereffects, or had I just gone stupid in my old age?

Max's momentary good humor was terminated with a look of anger.

"I cannot believe," he said, "that, after all the careful preparations we made, your performance could be so pathetically incompetent. Apparently, the minuscule talent I gave you credit for does not, in fact, exist."

Oh, now wait a second, said my brain. A glimmer had appeared in the mist.

Verified as Cassandra stood abruptly, her expression one of resentment.

Reaching up, she peeled away a wig, revealing dark hair underneath, an unmistakably male haircut.

Pulling free her blouse, she reached up underneath it, unfastened a front-hooking brassiere and yanked it down. The brassiere, I saw, was augmented by rubber pads.

She tossed it onto the chair.

But, of course, I can no longer say *she.*

For it was Brian Crane who stood before my son, his voice hoarse with anger as he snarled, *"Up yours, Max."*

With that, he strode into the entry hall, slamming the door behind him.

Then there was one.

Multiple questions crowded my mind, pounding for attention.

All quickly reduced to one, however.

Why had it all been done?

What was behind it?

It was maddening to me that Max did not come over to me and explain. I was there because he wanted me present, that was clear. But for what reason? He didn't explain the situation to me. What conceivable purpose could there have been in my being present throughout the entire mad charade?

Yet Max did not explain.

He didn't even look at me.

Instead, he stared at the door to the entry hall, his face impassive.

Leaving me immersed in drowning questions, none of them answerable.

After a while, he pushed slowly to his feet and trudged to the fireplace, his movements those of a man who more than felt his age and despair. Despite the agitation of confusion in my mind, I couldn't help but feel a pang of sorrow for his obvious distress.

He stood before the portrait of his long-dead wife.

The illumination in the room was so gloomy now that he switched on the light above the portrait.

The soft glow was cast down over Adelaide Delacorte's exquisite face.

Max stared at it, his expression one of suffering.

"It isn't true," he said. "I always loved you, Adelaide. *Always.*"

He drew in a trembling breath.

"I didn't know you were too ill to work that night," he told her. "I should have, but you know how I always am before a show, aware of nothing but the performance I'm about to give."

True, I could not help thinking.

Max twitched as a peal of thunder sounded. His face was whitened momentarily by a flash of lightning.

"Please," he said, "believe me. You should have *told* me. I would never have asked you to work if I'd had any idea how ill you were. You know that's true. Curse me for an oblivious fool, but it was an accident. An *accident*. I *swear* it."

He was unable to restrain a sob.

"Adelaide," he murmured. "Please. Forgive me."

He leaned against the fireplace for several minutes, lost in the agony of his remembrance and his guilt.

Then he straightened, teeth clenched, and switched off the light above the portrait.

Stepping over a pace, he reached up to one of the fireplace stones the Sheriff had examined visually, even touched.

He began to push on the stone.

Then he drew back his hand and turned to me.

He regarded me for several moments before walking over.

"It isn't right that you should see this, *Padre*," he said. "I've shocked you enough."

He began to push my wheelchair toward the entry hall.

My God, I thought, *after all this, are you going to withhold the goddam punch line?*

I wonder if I made a noise of protest, some faint sound which indicated the angry frustration I felt.

I'll never know.

All I do know is that Max stopped pushing me and gazed down at me, obviously thinking.

Tell me what is going on! pleaded my mind.

Did he pick up the plea telepathically? Who knows.

But he did change his mind.

"No," he said. "Shock or no shock, you have a right to know what's going on. It's only just, considering everything."

Was that a *smile*? It was extremely faint, and yet I could have sworn . . .

"Besides," he said, "I really want you to see the effect."

He turned my wheelchair toward the picture window.

Son, I thought, *aren't you going to tell me why you wanted Sheriff Plum to think that Brian was Cassandra?*

Not so. He left me sitting there as he returned to the fireplace. To that particular stone.

Which he pushed in all the way now.

I felt myself tighten (or did I?) as I heard a sound of machinery by the window overlooking the lake.

My God, I thought. *Blast my unseeing eyes. I've been a blind old fool. Taken in! And me* The Great Delacorte *before he was!*

Houdini performed the trick with much success. He called it *The Country Girl.*

It involved the impossible disappearance of a small girl sitting at a table near a window.

In Max's version of the effect, what appeared to be a window view of the gazebo by the lake wasn't that at all.

It was, in fact, a reflected view, created by double-sided mirrors in an addition built onto TMR.

For now, as the apparatus functioned, the view was altering, the gazebo and the lake disappearing from sight.

To be replaced by a freezer area approximately four feet wide and three feet deep, its height that of the window.

Inside the freezer area, suspended from a rope around her chest, was Cassandra Delacorte.

Her features stiff and white in death.

chapter 25

It was, of course, coincidence that, precisely at the moment Cassandra's corpse appeared to me, a roar of thunder cannonaded in the sky and lightning turned the awful sight into a tableau of blinding whiteness.

Max was unable to resist toasting the sky.

"Good timing!" he cried.

Outside, a torrent of rain began to fall, so heavy that it was, immediately, a curtain of descending water.

Max regarded the corpse of his wife.

There was no sense of triumph or of pleasure in his look.

"So," he said. "It worked."

It did not require the intellect of a Rhodes scholar to know what he meant.

With the help of Brian's talent at impersonating his sister, they had successfully fooled Harry.

And, more important, the Sheriff.

With all the tricks and counter-tricks occurring, Plum completely missed the main illusion of them all. (I missed it, too.)

The person he'd assumed to be Cassandra Delacorte wasn't her at all.

Max drained his glass of brandy and set down the glass.

He returned to me and placed a hand on my shoulder.

I know I shuddered then, for he felt it.

"I'm sorry, Father," he said. "Don't think I'm unaware of what I've done. I know that I've committed murder. Perhaps the motivation wasn't strong enough."

His voice hardened.

"I thought it *was*, though," he said.

He exhaled heavily.

"Now the final phase begins," he told me.

"The conclusion of the trick.

"I'll continue with the act. Not in Las Vegas, but in various other locations, jobs I'll arrange for myself. Las Vegas is too conspicuous. But lesser whereabouts will be in order.

"Where Brian's continued imitation of his sister will go unnoticed.

"The falling-out with Harry was, of course, essential.

"If Harry was around, he'd inevitably see through the pretense.

"Now he won't."

"*And,*" he went on, "Sheriff Plum 'keeping an eye' on me is equally essential.

"His value consists of the fact that he will, *at the same time*, be keeping an eye on the person he believes to be Cassandra, a witness to her ongoing existence."

And I thought he'd lost focus, the chilling idea came. How wrong I'd been. The discovery did nothing but dismay me further.

Did I wince as my son chuckled? I wanted to.

"Brother Brian's going to be a busy boy from now on," he said. "His 'gofer' days are over." He rubbed his eyes; he must have felt drained. "A busy boy, but not a happy one," he said.

He knelt beside my wheelchair.

"Not that he deserves to be happy," he said. "He has a lot of paying back to do for all those forged checks."

So that's it, I thought. *That's his hold on Brian.*

Max hissed scornfully.

"He was never very bright, was he?" he said.

"You know what I have in my safe, *Padre?* A contract signed by Brian.

"An agreement to assist me in the killing of his sister."

I closed my eyes to shut it all away. I couldn't bear these dreadful moments.

Max didn't notice.

"I had to insist on it, of course," he said.

He made a sound of dark amusement.

"After all," he went on, "could I trust the word of a man who'd help murder his own sister?"

Oh, God, Max, God. I wanted to weep.

Max made an odd sound, and I opened my eyes to look at him.

He was blinking his eyes. He closed them hard, then opened them again.

"I should have eaten something today," he said. "That much brandy on an empty stomach isn't good. But then, I have no appetite for food.

"Only for revenge," he finished.

Now he saw the look on my face; I guess I wasn't totally without expression.

"I know you think it was horrific what I did. It *is.* I *admit* it.

"But you never had this kind of motivation in your life.

"This kind of betrayal."

His right hand jerked up as though he meant to strike Cassandra, even dead.

"You don't know what she did to me," he said.

"Made me think that it was because of illness that my eyesight was failing, my hearing failing, my hand dexterity failing, my ability to concentrate on stage failing.

"*Even my ability to perform in bed,*" he finished in a low, venom-ridden voice.

His breath was quickening, his teeth on edge.

"Illness," he said. "That's what she had me believing.

"When all the time it was her.

"*Slowly poisoning me.*"

───

I stared at him in sickened dread. Not that he could see it, but I felt it.

Poisoning him?

Max shuddered with rage.

"She thought she could do it indefinitely," he said. "That I'd never find out.

"A *soupçon* of arsenic in my tea each day. A smidgen of it in my soup, my wine, my salad dressing.

"Just enough to keep me functioning, but weak enough so she could get control of the act. Dispose of my resistance without actually becoming a murderess."

He shouted at her suddenly, making me twitch.

"That's what you planned, wasn't it?" he said. "You stupid bitch! You'd have to have a live-in pharmacist to manage that! You were *killing* me, pure and simple!"

He shuddered again. "Control," he murmured. "Control."

The keystone of our professional and personal life.

How many times had I drummed *The Delacorte Motto* into his head?

"Do you understand now why I did it, *Padre?*" he asked, his voice controlled now.

I understand but can't condone, I thought. *You could have told the authorities. Poisoning is still a punishable crime.*

But that was overlooking pride, and pride's need for revenge.

And, being honest with myself, I could not say that, had the same thing been done to me in every respect, I would not have murdered for revenge also.

Like Adelaide, my Cara was an angel.

Had I been married to Cassandra, though . . .

I was taken from my darkened fantasy by Max's voice.

"Well, now you know," he said. "I regret, more than I can say, that you may have lost respect for me. But I do not regret the elimination of this adulterous, covetous, murderous *bitch.*"

Pushing to his feet, he walked to the fieldstone wall and pushed in the stone.

The machinery hummed, the freezer area began to close.

As it did, he glanced at it.

Stiffening with surprise, he started forward, then abruptly turned back and pushed in the stone again.

The machinery reversed itself; the freezer area began reopening.

Max moved over to it and stared at Cassandra.

What had he seen?

She hung motionless, her face a rigid, gray-white mask.

Max put on his glasses to look at her more closely.

What had he seen? My heartbeat slowly, heavily, was picking up momentum.

Max put his face closer to Cassandra's.

An icy hand clamping hard over my pulsing heart.

And Max recoiling with a gasp of shock.

Cassandra's right hand had twitched.

"No," said Max. I doubt if he was aware of speaking as he stared at her.

The hand was still. Cassandra hung immobile.

No, I thought, my mind-voice like my son's: incredulous, denying. It had only been a physical reaction. An involuntary muscle spasm caused by the contrast in temperatures between the room and the freezer.

It had to be.

Max swallowed dryly. Leaned in closer. Time stood still.

"If she isn't dead yet," he muttered.

He grimaced in fury.

"That idiot, Brian! If he's bungled *this!*"

Outside, the storm was increasing now, the sound of rainfall like that of heavy wind. The room was sunless, filled with shadows. *Turn on the light*, said a voice in my mind. A voice I hadn't heard for almost seventy years, that of a frightened boy.

Max was leaning in close. He *had* to know; I saw that. Closer and closer. He was very near the corpse's face now.

A strangled gasp tore from his throat as Cassandra's right hand, like a bloodless spider, jumped up, clutching at his jacket lapel.

I felt paralyzed by more than stroke effects now. I felt paralyzed with horror.

Max was slowly being drawn toward the corpse's face. Closer.

Closer.

Hitchingly, Cassandra's head raised up. *No!* a voice screamed in my mind.

Eyes staring, a gagging rattle in his throat, Max gaped at her.

The gray hand pulled him closer. Closer. Now his face was only inches from hers.

His breath choked off (with mine) as Cassandra's blood-shot eyes sprang open.

For an instant, they were staring at each other (as I felt death by shock approaching).

Then, with a demented cry, Max yanked back, tearing free of the leprous hand.

He lost balance and staggered backward, crashing down with a cry of pain as his elbows struck the hardwood floor.

A frozen observer, I watched in terror.

Cassandra had begun to twitch, her mouth working like that of a fish out of water.

Max tried to stand, but couldn't.

He pushed backward, staring at her.

Cassandra began to thrash against the rope like a frenzied animal.

Max watched, openmouthed, moans of impending madness pulsing in his throat.

The storm was increasing, thunder exploding in the sky, the darkened room sporadically illuminated as though blazing floodlights were being turned on, then off, lighting the hideous sight of Cassandra, eyes mad, pitching back and forth against the ropes.

Max tried again to stand. His legs would not support him.

Suddenly, he cried out, horrorstruck, as the rope pulled loose from one of the hooks and Cassandra's body flung forward, toppling from the freezer area onto the floor in front of Max. He jerked back with a hollow cry.

He had to stand or lose his mind. Straining every muscle, he pushed up to his knees, then wavered to his feet.

He had barely made it when Cassandra, her face a stiffened, frost-caked mask, lurched clumsily to her feet and came at him.

Crying out again, Max twisted around and staggered toward the entry hall, barely able to move, his balance failing.

He reached the door and fell against it, turning the knob with a shaking hand.

The door was locked.

With a sob of mindless dread, he jerked around to face her.

She was walking toward him like a poorly controlled marionette, her movements jerky, her head flopping from side to side.

The storm was at its peak now, thunder crashing deafeningly, lightning bleaching the frozen whiteness of Cassandra's face, her staring and unblinking eyes.

Shrieking with dread, Max lurched to his right to avoid her clutch, barely capable of movement.

He could go no more than several yards.

There, he collapsed to the floor, crying out in pain and horror.

He tried to stand, but couldn't.

Glassy-eyed, he lay on his back as Cassandra moved at him, expressionless and staring.

Max had trouble breathing. He made choking noises in his throat as he gaped up at the hideous figure looming over him.

With the last of his strength, he summoned forth a shriek of maddened fright, then lay there mutely, staring up at Cassandra, beyond response.

She stopped and looked down at him.

Thunder detonated. The room was blanched by lightning.

Then the hall door was unlocked, and Cassandra entered.

chapter 26

You've read the phrase: *His brain reeled,* haven't you?

It's a literal description, friends.

My brain reeled. The world had been upended. I could not think, only stare. Blankly.

As she'd come in, Cassandra had said (to Cassandra!), "That's enough."

And the corpse had looked around.

"That's *it?*" she said. "You didn't give me much time."

"There was enough," said living Cassandra.

"For you, maybe," responded corpse Cassandra.

And pulled off her wig.

Brian in white makeup.

◼▭

Max, unable to move, stared up at Brian.

As Cassandra exploded at her brother.

"What the hell was the idea of leaving me unconscious on the floor like that?" she demanded.

My brain mumbled *What?* Hadn't that been Brian made up as Cassandra?

Brian had exploded back at his sister.

"What the hell else could I do?" he cried. "Obviously, he put too much drug in that dart. I *tried* to bring you around, but I couldn't!

"And there was *no time!*" he ranted on. "I had to hide Harry in the cellar underneath the burial-case apparatus! Put that rubber mask over his head! Telephone the Sheriff! Make sure you were ready! Get into makeup and your clothes again! Be ready to be hanging in that goddam freezer! I hardly had all afternoon, did I?"

She did not relent.

"I thought Harry was really dead!" she raged.

"*Why?*" He looked confused. "You knew Max's plan! I told you every bit of it!"

"Well, I didn't know *that!*" she responded. "I thought—"

He cut her off, twisting around to look at me. "Can't we take him out of here?" he asked.

"Forget him!" she snarled. "*He's a cabbage!*"

"He's a helpless old man!" Brian cried.

"*Wrong!*" she said. "He's a goddam encumbrance, and I can't *wait* to get him out of here!"

(Merci, *Cassandra. Stay as sweet as you are.*)

"*Jesus God,*" she muttered angrily. "I had to go through that whole fucking charade thinking all the time that Harry was really dead."

Her voice was loud again.

"It threw me off completely!" she stormed. "It was a *nightmare!* I did *everything* wrong! If it hadn't been for Max's failing eyesight and hearing—"

Brian scowled.

"What the hell's the difference?" he said. "All's well that ends well, right?" His tone was bitter.

Cassandra regarded him tensely, then managed to control her temper.

With a forced smile, she moved to him and kissed him several times on the lips, her hands on his cheeks.

They were not sisterly kisses.

Which, doubling my bafflement, added (in a moment's time) an entirely new dimension to the lay of the land (if I may so refer to my daughter-in-law).

"*Fool*," she said to him in a chiding voice.

She slapped him lightly on the cheek.

"Now put him in the freezer, then get out of here."

He blew out a surrendering breath.

"Yes, ma'am," he murmured sadly.

Cassandra frowned at him. "What's wrong?"

"Nothing," he said. "Everything is peachy."

"You're not going to fall apart on me *now*, are you?" she asked. She gave him a Cassandra look.

"No, I'm not," he murmured.

"Well, do what you're told, then," she said.

"Sure."

She smiled and kissed him again. *Definitely* not a sisterly kiss.

Or a sisterly clutch at his groin.

"*Tonight*," she said.

Oh, what a tangled web, I thought as Brian turned away from her, Cassandra laughing softly.

He knelt beside Max and started to lift him up. Max's weight was dead, his limbs completely flaccid.

What have they done to him? I wondered.

"I can use that champagne now," Cassandra said.

She crossed to the bar as Brian, grunting from the effort, managed to lift Max to a standing position and began to half-drag, half-lead him toward the freezer.

He's still alive, I thought.

But completely helpless.

At the bar, Cassandra twirled the champagne bottle in the bucket, lifted it out and tore off its metallic neck wrapping.

Then she stopped and looked at the bottle.

Made a sound of grim amusement.

"What?" gasped Brian, using every bit of his strength to get Max to the freezer.

"If we could drug his private-stock brandy, chancing that he'd drink it of his own accord—as Harry did with the Scotch—how do we know Max didn't do the same thing with this bottle of champagne—so *conveniently* placed in the ice bucket? He could have used a hypo-needle, just as we did."

She dropped the bottle into the wastebasket.

"Good try, Max," she said.

The woman has no trust in anyone, I thought.

Opening the doors beneath the bar, she lifted out a new case of champagne and tore it open, removing one of its bottles. Tearing off its metallic seal, she started to thumb out the cork.

"Better to drink safe champagne on the rocks, eh *Padre?"* she said mockingly to me.

If I could only move, came the thought. *I would be able to kill.*

Hearing the pop of the cork and the brief gush of escaping liquid from the bottle, Brian looked around.

"Celebration time," he said glumly.

"Of course, love," she answered. "We have a lot to celebrate."

"Of course," said Brian.

"Oh, cheer up, for Christ's sake," Cassandra told him, pouring champagne into a glass of ice cubes.

Lifting the glass, she jiggled it for several moments, then drained it; sighed.

"Not as good as chilled," she said, "but it'll do."

Brian had Max to the freezer now and was putting him inside.

I watched, in pain.

"You really think he poisoned that champagne?" he asked, breathing hard.

"He could have," she answered, pouring herself a second drink. "He always planned ahead."

"What a twisted mind you have," he muttered.

"Twisted, but surviving," she told him, taking a sip of her second drink.

She raised her glass toastingly toward the freezer.

"You're right, Max," she said. "It *is* my favorite brand. Not the exact bottle of it that you'd planned on. However—as brother Brian put it—all's well that ends well."

Oh God, I'd be able to kill! I thought, enraged.

Now Max sagged in the same spot where he'd thought his dead wife had been hanging minutes earlier.

I felt myself grow tense as his lips stirred laboredly.

"The brandy?" he asked in a faint voice.

"Oh, you didn't hear me, darling?" Cassandra said lightly. "Yes, of course. The brandy."

"The same stuff she's been putting in your food for thirteen months," Brian added.

"Shut up," Cassandra told him.

"A lot more of it, though," Brian said.

"*Shut up,*" she ordered.

I closed my eyes. *If I could only vanish from this awful place,* I thought. *Be an Effect—be gone in a flash.* I hated what was going on and what had gone on. All of it was sickening, dismaying. How could it have gone so far?

Finished with Max, Brian bowed toward my son.

"*Salud,* Great Delacorte," he said. "You should have given me more credit than you did."

"Get out of here and change," Cassandra told him.

"Yes, ma'am."

Turning on his heel, he crossed to the entry hall and left.

I watched Cassandra as she gazed at Max.

Is this the end, then?

Of me as well as Max, it occurred to me. She'd want me out of the house now. Out of her life.

More than likely, out of the world.

What was one less vegetable to her?

Now she spoke. Did it bother her that I could hear—or did she *want* me to hear?

Maybe my presence didn't even occur to her as she spoke to Max.

"You *should* have given him more credit," she said.

She shook her head in disbelief.

"Did you really think he'd help you *murder* me?

"Just because you had those forged checks?

"The way he feels about me?"

She drained her glass and sighed with pleasure, smiling.

Lewdly, let me make it clear.

"But then, you never knew about that, did you?" she said. "Never knew it wasn't only Harry I was 'bedding,' as you so slyly put it."

She made a sound of contempt.

"I had no intention that you'd know, of course," she told him.

Returning to the bar, she poured her glass full of champagne again. And I began to feel a kind of dark peace, knowing that Max and I would soon be free of this defilement.

chapter 27

Another sound of contempt from Cassandra now, this one more intense.

"You were so *certain* it was Brian imitating me in order to fool the Sheriff," she said.

"True, the poison had weakened your eyesight and your hearing.

"But it was *more* than that. We both know that, don't we?

"*It was your ego.*

"Your damned, incredible ego.

"You'd *planned* it that way. Ergo, *it must be happening that way.*

"*The Great Delacorte* never makes a mistake."

A scoffing laugh.

"Even though I gave myself away a dozen times," she continued, "lost control completely when I saw that goddam shrine to goddam Adelaide."

She pointed a shaking finger at him.

"You can bet your dying ass I'll soon get rid of *that*," she told him fiercely.

She shook her head, amused again.

"You didn't notice it," she said. "Even though I had to wear a wig over a wig over my hair. My *God.*

"Even though I had to wear a pair of falsies over my own taped-down tits."

She glanced at me, grinning. "Sorry, *Daddy,*" she said. "Didn't mean to offend."

She looked back at Max again.

"I couldn't have been more transparent," she said. "But you were sure that it was Brian, so you *saw* Brian, you *heard* Brian."

She hissed. *"Idiot,"* she muttered.

She glanced at me again. "Your son is an idiot!" she cried. *"Padre."*

She walked over to the freezer, taking the bottle and glass with her.

"Sorry your little plot didn't work," she said. *"But,* the well-laid plans—" Smiling, she took a long sip of champagne.

"And now the final phase of *my* scenario," she went on.

"Maximilian Delacorte—the *Great*—takes a trip to the Caribbean to recover from an illness which was ruining his career; lots of witnesses to *that.*

"He charters a yacht, starts drinking heavily, then one night falls overboard and disappears."

She snickered.

"And Brian swims for a while until I pick him up."

Another snicker.

"You didn't know that he can imitate you, too. Not as well as he can imitate me, but good enough to fool some strangers into testifying to Maximilian Delacorte's unhappy demise. Was it suicide? Perhaps."

She grinned. "The poor man was so depressed about his failing career," she said.

She chuckled.

"Then, of course, I might not pick up Brian after all," she said. *"I might just let him drown."*

She is *a hellhag*, I thought. I understood exactly why my son had wanted to kill her.

I would have wanted the same.

"If I *do* pick him up," Cassandra was continuing, "I'll damn well keep him in his place, the same way you were doing it—with those forged checks, that murder contract."

She chuckled again; again, lewdly.

"Not that he'd ever turn on me," she said. "I've handled him all my life."

Her eyes hooded sensuously.

"In more ways than one," she said.

What is Max thinking about all this? I wondered.

Or was he still *capable* of thought? Had the poison deprived him of all capacity by then?

Cassandra had taken another drink, and she sighed contentedly.

"Anyway, what matters is that I have your effects now," she said. "I can do what I please with them. Create a new act. A *today* act. One that will sell."

She giggled softly. Yes, dear reader, *giggled.*

"I may even let Harry be my booking agent," she said. She bared her teeth.

"And *screw* him when I feel the urge," she added.

If only I could move, I thought.

Pathetically.

Max was looking at her, his expression one of (almost gentle!) condemnation.

"Don't look at me like that," she said.

"This didn't have to happen.

"We could have worked together. Or, at least, I thought we could have, until I saw that shrine.

"I couldn't believe the anger it made me feel—the pain.

"Yes, pain! I thought you'd lost the power to hurt me

long ago. The power to make me care about anything that had to do with us."

I felt my body tightening as Max *replied.*

"I would . . . hardly . . . think you cared . . . at all . . . when you were . . . *poisoning* me for . . . thirteen months," he managed to get out.

"You're right," she agreed, trying to act as though the sound of his voice had not unnerved her.

"I *never* cared for you," she said, "only for your success. *"And now I've got it."*

— — —

She poured herself another glassful of champagne and held it up.

"To *me*," she said. *"The New Great Delacorte."*

Never! I thought, absurdly.

Cassandra emptied the glass, then walked over to the desk, set the bottle and glass on top of it, and moving to the fieldstone wall, pushed in the stone. The apparatus began to close.

Cassandra looked at her dying husband.

"See you in hell," she said.

Max smiled. (How *could* he?)

"It's a date," he responded.

With his remaining strength, he chuckled as the freezer folded in on itself until, once more, I saw only the picture window overlooking the gazebo by the lake.

The storm was decreasing now, moving off, the rain slackening, thunder and lightning almost negligible. A coincidence?

Or had Nature taken notice and reduced its accompanying violence as the violence in the room subsided?

Cassandra looked at me.

"We'll deal with you anon," she told me. "Maybe put you in the freezer with your son."

A dazzling smile. "We'll see, old man," she said.

She started toward the entry hall.

She was almost to the doorway when from a corner of her eyes, she saw (as I did) a movement on the surface of the globe.

She stopped and turned around, looking in that direction.

The outer layer of the globe was rolling downward, revealing the glass globe underneath. *Harry's head again?* I thought. What would be the point of that?

Max's.

His lips drawn back in an amiable smile.

"While I realize," he said, "that the chance of your ever seeing this is small indeed, at the same time, I have taken the precaution, as a good magician should, of preparing an alternative ending."

Despite my grief, I felt a glow of warmth at that. He'd never forgotten.

"Accordingly, I have injected through the cork and wrapping of the apparently unopened bottle in the ice bucket a tasteless, slow-acting but extremely efficacious poison."

Cassandra started. Then her lips jerked back in a barking laugh of triumph.

"You really *did* poison it, you son of a bitch," she said.

"In addition," Max's head went on, "I have also injected the same poison into every champagne bottle under the bar—resealing the cases, of course.

"This in the event that you suspect the bottle in the ice bucket and use another one."

Cassandra stiffened with dread. While in the heart of the ancient vegetable, a cheer erupted. *Bravo, Sonny!*

"I know you love your favorite champagne after any kind of personal triumph," Max's head continued.

He paused.

"Not that you will ever have the chance to drink it," he said. "You'll be hanging in the freezer, dead. Still—"

The head smiled cunningly.

"*—who knows?*" it said.

It was either a choice coincidence or (more likely) the burst of shock which had flooded her system that caused Cassandra to feel the poison for the first time at that very moment.

She began to weave, one hand pressed against her stomach.

"*No,*" she said.

She stared in unbelieving shock at Max's head as it completed its statement.

"If it comes to it, however," it said, "*bon voyage,* Cassandra. Despite your wondrous machinations—whatever they have been, and I'm sure they were impressive—you have lost the game, as well as I."

As Cassandra gaped at the head, the outer layer of the globe rolled back up, and once again it was an antique image of the world.

Cassandra tried to make it to the telephone.

She couldn't. Her legs began to lose the power to support her.

"Brian!" she called. "*Brian!*"

She lurched toward the desk, but never reached it, instead pitching forward to the floor.

There she lay gasping, legs drawn up, agony stabbing at her insides. (It seemed apparent by the way she clutched at her stomach.)

I doubt if, in all that pain, she could have summoned a single thought about her husband's final victory.

And I doubt that I could ever have killed her. I felt too sorry for her.

And her wasted life.

What else could I do?

It was over. Nothing more could possibly take place.

And yet it did.

Both Cassandra's eyes and mine moved to the desk chair.
It was turning by itself.
It stood there, reversed, for several moments.
Then a curl of white smoke drifted upward from behind its back.
Cassandra gaped at it. I gaped at it.
How could Max possibly be alive?

The chair turned back.
My brain felt numb.
Sitting in it, smoking a cigar, was Sheriff Plum.
Cassandra made a sound of dazed confusion. She could make no sense whatever of the Sheriff's appearance. Nor could I.
Still, he might save her life!
"Help me," she asked in a feeble voice.
The Sheriff only stared at her.
"Guess you won't be going back to Harry Kendal now," he said, "or letting your brother drown at sea."
She obviously didn't comprehend what he was saying. *"Please,"* she begged.
"Looks like you and the Mister have killed each other off," he said.
His eyes were like stones.
"Leaving everything to *Padre,"* he said. "And to whoever takes care of *Padre."*
He rose from the chair and walked around the desk.
Cassandra gasped.
From the waist up, he was wearing Sheriff Plum's clothes.
From the waist down, Cassandra's.
Her mouth fell open as she understood.
Too late.

Brian came over and, kneeling, checked for her pulse beat.

There was none; she was gone.

He put her hand back down on the floor and stared at her.

Then sobbed.

"Did you ever care for *anyone?*" he asked.

He pressed his left hand over his eyes and began to cry harder.

I don't know how long he wept. It was a good while, though.

Finally, rubbing dry his eyes and cheeks, he drew in a long, bracing breath of air and stood.

Moving to the desk, he picked up the telephone and pressed the Operator button.

As he waited, he began to peel away his Sheriff disguise.

"The Sheriff's office, please," he said. "This is an emergency."

He continued peeling off the disguise while he waited again.

Finally, the Sheriff's office answered. Brian asked for Plum and was connected.

"Sheriff Plum," he said. "My name is Brian Crane. I'm calling from the house of Maximilian and Cassandra Delacorte on Medfield Road. Can you come here right away?"

He looked, stricken, at his dead sister.

"There's been a tragedy," he said.

chapter 28

Brian sat in silence for at least ten minutes, idly picking at the remainder of his Sheriff Plum facial disguise. He seemed to stare into his thoughts; never had I felt more invisible.

Rising finally, he took off the Sheriff's shirt, revealing, underneath, Cassandra's pink blouse, which he also removed, revealing a sweat-laved T-shirt underneath. He took off the skirt he'd worn, the shoes and stockings. Beneath the skirt, he wore the trousers of Sheriff Plum.

Still, he did not look at me, his face expressionless. Whatever thoughts he had were so buried, they were not reflected, even for an instant, on his face.

Barefoot, he moved to where Cassandra lay and looked down at her.

Abruptly, his face revealed all: incredulous sorrow, anguish so complete it appeared as though he might lose control.

He slumped to his knees beside her, taking hold of her

limp right hand. The sob that broke in his chest wracked his entire body.

"*Why?*" he asked, scarcely able to speak the word.

His head bowed and he wept again; for the sister he had loved so deeply, yet had made no effort to save.

At last he raised his head and looked at me, eyes glistening.

"You never knew about us, did you, *Padre?*" he said. "You only knew what Max told you and what little you saw."

Slowly and gently, he stroked his sister's hand as he spoke.

"Our father was an alcoholic," he said. "A failed vaudevillian who didn't mellow with inebriation but turned vicious instead. Abused our mother and us." He bared his teeth momentarily. "And, in Cassandra's case . . ."

He didn't finish, but he didn't have to; I understood.

"When I was ten, my mother hanged herself," he went on. "Cassandra took her place in my life, the only person in the world I could trust.

"She took me away from our father when she was sixteen and I was thirteen. By then, she'd made up her mind to follow no rules but to do anything she could to get ahead.

"I didn't blame her; I don't blame her now. We were two of a kind—angry, vengeful, pitted against a world which had given us nothing but pain.

"So we became what you saw and heard about from Max—a pair of icy opportunists. Not that he knew it at first. Cassandra was too good at pretending to allow him to see what she—and I—really were."

He stopped speaking and lowered his head again; I thought he was finished.

He wasn't. Rising, he retrieved the skirt he'd removed and lay it across Cassandra's still features.

Then he moved to the picture window and stared out at the lake, a faint smile on his lips. *Is he thinking,* I wondered, *that the view he sees is only a reflection?* I had no way of knowing.

Finally, he turned and walked to the desk, sitting on its edge.

"We have a little wait, don't we?" he said.

"Where was I?"

He stared at me bleakly; then, after several moments, he spoke again.

"She had an affair with a stage magician when she was seventeen. She used him to learn his trade and she taught me what she'd learned.

"Then she dropped him, and it was the two of us again, together in . . . every way," he murmured.

His smile was bitter.

"Several other 'status-enhancing'—as she called them—relationships followed before she met Max and set her cap for him. Moving in after Adelaide's death. With me, as always, trailing behind, her faithful lapdog . . . slavish to her every demand."

He sighed heavily.

"Things changed after they were married," he said. "My closeness to her gradually deteriorated. She was—without my knowing it—scheming toward a future which did not include me.

"I tried not to notice it. I'd been trained to trust her totally, believe her every word. I *loved* her, *Padre*—" His voice broke, and he had to pause to regain himself.

"But in spite of that," he said, "I had to recognize, eventually, that I was living—in her life, at least—on borrowed time."

―――

"It all came to a head when Max demanded that I help him eliminate her because of what she was doing to him."

The bitter smile again.

"How clever she was," he said. "Until that moment, I'd had no idea that she was plotting either Max's dissolution as a performer or—if that didn't work—his death.

"Discovering that was a traumatic blow to me, *Padre*," he went on. "Putting aside everything we'd meant to one another, she was planning to betray me.

"I saw the cabal; Cassandra and Harry versus Max, with me completely out of the picture.

"It was then that the lapdog planned his revenge."

―――

"I pretended to agree with Max. Even signed that stupid murder contract with him; of course, I planned to destroy it later.

"Then I told Cassandra what he was planning to do: drug her with the blowgun dart and have me hang her in the freezer to die slowly—as she planned to let *him* die slowly from arsenic poisoning."

Once more, that bitter smile.

"She pretended, of course, that she'd always intended to tell me what she'd been doing," he said.

He turned his head and looked at Cassandra's body, his expression once again unreadable. He stared at her for more than a minute.

Then he murmured, *"Right,"* and moved behind the desk. Sitting, he took a sheet of paper from the drawer and began to write on it.

"They all misread me, *Padre*," he said. "Brian the pathetic gofer. Nothing but a pawn to be moved around their murderous chessboard."

His expression was hard now, his voice angry.

"They should have given me more credit," he said.

"I made fools of them both.

"Pretending to help each one separately, I played my game and stood by while they contrived to murder one another."

He shuddered.

"Not that I intended for her to die," he said. "Max surprised me there. And my own anger at what I heard her say while I was behind the wall panel—that she might let me drown at sea—so enraged me that . . ."

His breath faltered.

"I might have saved her," he said. "Then again, maybe there wasn't time; I'll never know.

"So—in my total rage—I let her know what I'd done. Then I let her die."

Another faltering breath. He had to stop writing, his hand shook so badly.

A minute later, he put the pen back into its holder.

"Why have I told you all this?" he inquired.

He made a sound of dark amusement.

"Probably because you're the only audience I'll ever have.

"The perfect audience in one respect; you can't fidget in your seat or walk out. You have to listen to every word.

"At the same time, the worst audience I could ever have because you can't react, you can't respond in any way. Applause? Forget it. A cheer? No way. The audience participation of a cabbage is limited. Forgive me for saying so, *Padre*.

I always liked you, and respected you for what you'd done with your life. But as an *audience* . . ." He shook his head.

Little did he know.

There was complete reaction. And response, if only inwardly.

No gofer he. Instead, a diabolically clever man who'd played a two-sided game against Cassandra and my son.

Neither of them conceived, you see, that he was capable of such an ingeniously sinister plot against them. Blinded by their confident assumptions, they never noticed that, while each of them was involved in his (and her) intricate scheme, Brian was outmaneuvering them both.

He had even dared to call attention to himself by portraying the Sheriff as a slow-witted rustic!

Did he experience some sense of dreadful glee at that deception?

Brian stood and walked to the bar.

Removing the champagne bottle from its ice bucket, he poured a glassful and drank it in a swallow.

I wondered if my face betrayed the utter shock I felt.

"Don't worry, *Padre*," he said. "I've left a written confession on the desk."

He chuckled.

"Not that it's likely they'll think you did it all. Still . . ."

He winced as the poison began to take effect.

Face set, he poured himself another glassful, raised it toward me in a final toast.

"*Prosit, Padre*," he said. "And farewell."

He drained the glass and put it back on the bar.

Moving to where Cassandra's body lay, he stretched himself out beside her and took her hand in his. He made a sound of pain. Then, chillingly, he laughed.

"The real Sheriff Plum has got a lot to deal with here," he said.

He closed his eyes.

"Good luck, *Padre*," he murmured.

Then he, too, was gone.

I complete the tale as expeditiously as possible.

Sheriff Plum arrived soon after—looking more like an un-bearded Abraham Lincoln than the portly figure Brian had presented—and took over. Unlike Brian's characterization of him, he was a man of sharp perception.

The case was closed in due time. Later on, I caught up with the months of newspaper, magazine, tabloid, and television coverage of the case.

The court allowed me to retain the full estate, the servants remaining to take care of me.

Then an odd—and wholly unexpected—thing occurred.

The vegetable made a comeback.

Medical opinion varied, but the consensus was that the shock of witnessing the horrors of that afternoon—while being totally unable to stop them in any way—had traumatized my system.

Whether this is true or not, I'll never know.

All I do know is that for some fortuitous reason, my arterial blood flow discovered an alternate route to the damaged area of my brain, effecting a gradual but definite recovery.

Not complete, of course. I won't be vying in future Olympic Games.

Still, I'm well enough, at eighty-seven, to get about a little, feed myself, manage bathroom matters unassisted (there's a pleasure, let me tell you!), and write about what happened that day.

A minor coda to the story.

My son's estate was not extensive, most of it being invested in the house.

Accordingly, in order to acquire living funds, I had to sell the house.

I did so with little reluctance; it was filled with too many painful memories. I sold it furnished. And to whom?

How utterly ironic—

Harry.

He had always coveted the place, you see. No doubt he thought it grimly satisfying to be able to possess it after the way Max had tormented him there.

His offer was the highest among a scarce few bidders.

So I had to sell it to him.

Before I left, however, I called in a local handyman and had the entire place rewired so that every time Harry turned on a lamp or pushed up a light switch or tried to use an electric appliance, breaker switches were thrown. My one regret was that the house didn't still use screw-in fuses.

Better still (I had to pay the handyman a tidy sum to keep his mouth shut on this), I had every screw in every door and cabinet hinge in the house removed, the screw holes injected with hydrochloric acid, then the screws tightened back in place.

I will carry to my grave the heartwarming vision of that amoral sleazeball having every door and cabinet face fall off, one by one, in his hands as the acid did its work!

Me?

I live in St. John. Always loved the place since my wife and I had stayed there on numerous vacations.

A jolly Irish woman named Endira Muldoon (thrice widowed, with nine children and seventeen grandchildren scattered about the globe) comes every day to my cottage to cook and provide for me.

Each day she drives me to the beach—unless there is a hurricane, of course, in which case I remain at home.

I've collected a group of young children who gather around me on the sand while I perform minor hand manipulations for them. Colored balls and handkerchiefs, disappearances and replications, mostly.

They seem to enjoy it.